IONICA

CONTENTS

NOTE

William Johnson published in 1858 a slender volume bound in green cloth, (Smith, Elder & Co.) which was entitled "Ionica," and which comprised forty-eight poems.

In 1877 he printed privately a little paper-covered book (Cambridge University Press), entitled "Ionica II," containing twenty-five poems. This book is a rare bibliographical curiosity. It has neither titlepage nor index; it bears no author's name; and it is printed without punctuation, on a theory of the author's, spaces being left, instead of stops, to indicate pauses.

In 1891 he published a book, "Ionica" (George Allen), which contained most of the contents of the two previous volumes, together with some pieces not previously published—eighty-five poems in all.

The present volume is a reprint of the 1891 volume; but it has been thought well to include, in an appendix, certain of the poems which appeared in one or other of the first two issues, but were omitted from the 1891 issue, together with a little Greek lyric, with its English equivalent, from the "Letters and Journals."

The poems from page 1 to page 104, Desiderato to All that was possible, appeared in the 1858 volume, together with those on pages 211 to 216, To the Infallible, The Swimmer's Wish, and An Apology. The poems from page 105 to page 162, Scheveningen Avenue to L'Oiseau Bleu, appeared in the 1877 volume, together with those on pages 217 and 218, Notre Dame and In Honour of Matthew Prior. The remainder of the poems, from page 163 to page 210, appeared in the 1891 volume for the first time. The dates subjoined to the poems are those which he himself added, and indicate the date of composition.

INTRODUCTION

WILLIAM CORY (Johnson) was born at Torrington in Devonshire, on January 9, 1823. He was the son of Charles William Johnson, a merchant, who retired at the early age of thirty, with a modest competence, and married his cousin, Theresa Furse, of Halsdon, near Torrington, to whom he had long been attached. He lived a quiet, upright, peaceable life at Torrington, content with little, and discharging simple, kindly, neighbourly duties, alike removed from ambition and indolence. William Cory had always a deep love of his old home, a strong sense of local sanctities and tender associations. "I hope you will always feel," his mother used to say, "wherever you live, that Torrington belongs to you." He said himself, in later years, "I want to be a Devon man and a Torrington man." His memory lingered over the vine-shaded verandah, the jessamine that grew by the balustrade of the steps, the broad-leaved myrtle that covered the wall of the little yard.

The boy was elected on the foundation at Eton in 1832, little guessing that it was to be his home for forty years. He worked hard at school, became a first-rate classical scholar, winning the Newcastle Scholarship in 1841, and being elected Scholar of King's in 1842. He seems to have been a quiet, retiring boy, with few intimate friends, respected for his ability and his courtesy, living a self-contained, bookish life, yet with a keen sense of school patriotism—though he had few pleasant memories of his boyhood.

Honours came to him fast at Cambridge. He won the Chancellor's English Medal with a poem on Plato in 1843, the Craven Scholarship in 1844. In those days Kingsmen did not enter for the Tripos, but received a degree, without examination, by ancient privilege. He succeeded to a Fellowship in 1845, and in the same year was appointed to a Mastership at Eton by Dr. Hawtrey. At Cambridge he seems to have read widely, to have thought much, and to have been interested in social questions. Till that time he had been an unreflecting Tory and a strong High Churchman, but he now adopted more Liberal principles, and for the rest of his life was a convinced Whig. The underlying principle of Whiggism, as he understood it, was a firm faith in human reason. Thus, in a letter of 1875, he represents the Whigs as saying to their adversaries, "You are in a majority now: if I were an ultra-democrat or counter of noses, I should submit to you as having a transcendental—sometimes called divine— right; if I were a redcap, I should buy dynamite and blow you up; if I were a Tory, I should go to church or to bed; as it is, I go to work to turn your majority into a minority. I shall do it by reasoning and by attractive virtue." He intended in his university days, and for some time after, to take Anglican Orders, though he had also some thought of going to the Bar; but he accepted a Mastership with much relief, with the hope, as he wrote in an early letter, "that before my time is out, I may rejoice in having turned out of my pupil-room perhaps one brave soldier, or one wise historian, or one generous legislator, or one patient missionary." The whole of his professional life, a period of twenty-seven years, was to be spent at Eton.

No one who knew William Cory will think it an exaggeration to say that his mind was probably one of the most vigorous and commanding minds of the century. He had a mental equipment of the foremost order, great intellectual curiosity, immense vigour and many-sidedness, combined with a firm grasp of a subject, perfect clearness of thought, and absolute lucidity of expression.

He never lost sight of principles among a crowd of details; and though he had a strong bias in certain directions, he had a just and catholic appreciation even of facts which told against his case. Yet his knowledge was never dry or cold; it was full to the brim of deep sentiment and natural feeling.

He had a wide knowledge of history, of politics, both home and foreign, of political economy, of moral science. Indeed, he examined more than once in the Moral Science Tripos at Cambridge.

He had a thorough acquaintance with and a deep love of literature; and all this in spite of the fact that he lived a very laborious and wearing life as a school-teacher, with impossibly large classes, and devoted himself with whole-hearted enthusiasm to his profession. His knowledge was, moreover, not mere erudition and patient accumulation. It was all ready for use, and at his fingers' ends. Moreover, he combined with this a quality, which is not generally found in combination with the highly-developed faculties of the doctrinaire, namely an intense and fervent emotion. He was a lover of political and social liberty, a patriot to the marrow of his bones; he loved his country with a passionate devotion, and worshipped the heroes of his native land, statesmen, soldiers, sailors, poets, with an ardent adoration; the glory and honour of England were the breath of his nostrils. Deeds of heroism, examples of high courage and noble self-sacrifice, were the memories that thrilled his heart. As a man of fifty he wept over Lanfrey's account of Nelson's death; he felt our defeat at Majuba Hill like a keen personal humiliation; his letter on the subject is as the words of one mourning for his mother.

But his was not a mere poetical emotion, supplying him with highly-coloured rhetoric, or sentimental panegyric. He had a technical and minute acquaintance with the detailed movement of wars, the precise ships and regiments engaged, the personalities and characters of commanders and officers, the conduct of the rank and file.

Many delightful stories remain in the memories of his friends and hearers to attest this. His pupil-room at Eton, in what was formerly the old Christopher Inn, was close to the street, and the passage of the Guards through Eton, to and from their Windsor quarters, is an incident of constant occurrence. When the stately military music was heard far off, in gusty splendour, in the little town, or the fifes and drums of some detachment swept blithely past, he would throw down his pen and go down the little staircase to the road, the boys crowding round him. "Brats, the British army!" he would say, and stand, looking and listening, his eyes filled with gathering tears, and his heart full of proud memories, while the rhythmical beat of the footsteps went briskly echoing by.

Again, he went down to Portsmouth to see a friend who was in command of a man-of-war; he was rowed about among the hulks; the sailors in the gig looked half contemptuously at the sturdy landsman, huddled in a cloak, hunched up in the stem-sheets, peering about through his spectacles. But contempt became first astonishment, and then bewildered admiration, when they found that he knew the position of every ship, and the engagements in which each had fought.

He was of course a man of strong preferences and prejudices; he thought of statesmen and patriots, such as Pitt, Nelson, Castlereagh, Melbourne, and Wellington, with an almost personal affection. The one title to his vehement love was that a man should have served his country, striven to enhance her greatness, extended her empire, and safeguarded her liberty.

It was the same with his feeling for authors. He loved Virgil as a friend; he almost worshipped Charlotte Brontë. He spoke of Tennyson as "the light and joy of my poor life." In 1868 he saw Sir W. Scott's portrait in London, and wrote: "Sir Walter Scott, shrewd yet wistful, boyish yet dry, looking as if he would ask and answer questions of the fairies—him I saw through a mist of weeping. He is my lost childhood, he is my first great friend. I long for him, and hate the death that parts us."

In literature, the first claim on his regard was that a writer should have looked on life with a high-hearted, generous gaze, should have cared intensely for humanity, should have hoped, loved, suffered, not in selfish isolation, but with eager affection. Thus he was not only a philosophical historian, nor a mere technical critic; he was for ever dominated by an intense personal fervour. He cared little for the manner of saying a hing, so long as the heart spoke out frankly and freely; he strove to discern the energy of the soul in all men; he could forgive everything except meanness, cowardice, egotism and conceit; there was no fault of a generous and impulsive nature that he could not condone.

Thus he was for many boys a deeply inspiring teacher; he had the art of awakening enthusiasm, of investing all he touched with a mysterious charm, the charm of wide and accurate knowledge illuminated by feeling and emotion. He rebuked ignorance in a way which communicated the desire to know. There are many men alive who trace the fruit and flower of their intellectual life to his generous and free-handed sowing. But in spite of the fact that the work of a teacher of boys was intensely congenial to him, that he loved generous boyhood, and tender souls, and awakening minds with all his heart, he was not wholly in the right place as an instructor of youth. With all his sympathy for what was weak and immature, he was yet impatient of dullness, of stupidity, of caution; much that he said was too mature, too exalted for the cramped and limited minds of boyhood. He was sensitive to the charm of eager, high-spirited, and affectionate natures, but he had also the equable, just, paternal interest in boys which is an essential quality in a wise schoolmaster. Yet he was apt to make favourites; and though he demanded of his chosen pupils and friends a high intellectual zeal, though he was merciless to all sloppiness and lack of interest, yet he forfeited a wider influence by his reputation for partiality, and by an obvious susceptibility to grace of manner and unaffected courtesy. Boys who did not understand him, and whom he did not care to try to understand, thought him simply fanciful and eccentric. It is perhaps to be regretted that unforeseen difficulties prevented his being elected Tutor of his old College, and still more that in 1860 he was passed over in favour of Kingsley, when the Prime Minister, Lord Palmerston, submitted his name to the Queen for the Professorship of Modern History at Cambridge. Four men were suggested, of whom Blakesley and Venables refused the post. Sir Arthur Helps was set aside, and it would have been offered to Johnson, if the Prince Consort had not

17

suggested Kingsley. Yet Johnson would hardly have been in his right place as a teacher of young men. He would have been, on the one hand, brought into contact with more vigorous and independent minds, capable of appreciating the force and width of his teaching, and of comprehending the quality and beauty of his enthusiasms. But, on the other hand, he was too impatient of any difference of opinion, and, though he loved equal talk, he hated argument. And after all, he did a great work at Eton; for nearly a quarter of a century he sent out boys who cared eagerly and generously for the things of the mind.

A second attempt was made, in 1869, to get him appointed to the history professorship, but Seeley was considered to have a better claim. Writing to a friend on the subject, Johnson said: "I am not learned. I don't care about history in the common meaning of the word."

It is astonishing to see in his Diaries the immense trouble he took to awaken interest among his pupils. He was for ever trying experiments; he would read a dozen books to enable him to give a little scientific lecture, for he was one of the first to appreciate the educational value of science; he spent money on chemical apparatus, and tried to interest the boys by simple demonstrations. His educational ideals can best be seen in an essay full of poetical genius, on the education of the reasoning faculties, which he contributed to the "Essays on a Liberal Education," edited in 1867 by F. W. Farrar. Any one who wishes to understand Johnson's point of view, should study this brilliant and beautiful discourse. It is not only wise and liberal, but it is intensely practical, besides containing a number of suggestive and poetical thoughts.

He loved his Eton life more and more every year. As with Eumelus of Corinth, "dear to his heart was the muse that has the simple lyre and the sandals of freedom." He took refuge, as it became clear to him that his wider ambitions could not be realised, that he would not set the mark he might have set upon the age, in a "proud unworldliness," in heightened and intensified emotion. He made many friendships. He taught, as the years went on, as well or better than ever; he took great delight in the society of a few pupils and younger colleagues; but a shadow fell on him; he began to feel his strength unequal to the demands upon it; and he made a sudden resolution to retire from his Eton work.

He had taken some years before, as a house for his holidays, Halsdon, a country place near his native Torrington, which belonged to his brother, Archdeacon Wellington Furse of Westminster, who had changed his name from Johnson to Furse, on succeeding to the property of an uncle. Here he retired, and strove to live an active and philosophical life, fighting bravely with regret, and feeling with sensitive sorrow the turning of the sweet page. He tried, too, to serve and help his simple country neighbours, as indeed he had desired to do even at Eton, by showing them many small, thoughtful, and unobtrusive kindnesses, just as his father had done. But he lived much, like all poetical natures, in tender retrospect; and the ending of the bright days brought with it a heartache that even nature, which he worshipped like a poet, was powerless to console. But he loved his woods and sloping fields, and the clear river passing under its high banks through deep pools. It served to remind him sadly of his beloved Thames, the green banks fringed with comfrey and loosestrife, the drooping willows, the cool smell of the weedy weir; of glad hours of light-hearted enjoyment with his boy-companions, full of blithe gaiety and laughter.

After a few years, he went out to Madeira, where he married a wife much younger than himself, Miss Rosa Caroline Guille, daughter of a Devonshire clergyman; and at Madeira his only son was born, whom he named Andrew, because it was a name never borne by a Pope, or, as he sometimes said, "by a sneak." He devoted himself at this time to the composition of two volumes of a "Guide to Modern English History." But his want of practice in historical writing is here revealed, though it must be borne in mind that it was originally drawn up for the use of a Japanese student. The book is full of acute perceptions, fine judgments, felicitous epigrams—but it is too allusive, too fantastic; neither has it the balance and justice required for so serious and comprehensive a task.

At the same time the learning it displays is extraordinary. It was written almost without books of reference, and out of the recollections of a man of genius, who remembered all that he read, and considered reading the newspaper to be one of the first duties of life.

Cory's other writings are few. Two little educational books are worth mentioning: a book of Latin prose exercises, called *Nuces*, the sentences of which are full of recondite allusions, curious humour, and epigrammatic expression; and a slender volume for teaching Latin lyrics, called *Lucretilis*, the exercises being literally translated from the Latin originals which he first composed. *Lucretilis* is not only, as Munro said, the most Horatian verse ever written since Horace, but full of deep and pathetic poetry. Such a poem as No. xxvii., recording the abandoning of Hercules by the Argonauts, is intensely autobiographical. He speaks, in a parable, of the life of Eton going on without him, and of his faith in her great future:

> "sed Argo
> Vela facit tamen, aureumque
>
> "Vellus petendum est. Tiphys ad hoc tenet
> Clavum magister; stat Telamon vigil,
> Stat Castor in prora, paratus
> Ferre maris salientis ictus."

After some years in Madeira, he came back to England and settled in Hampstead; his later days were clouded with anxieties and illness. But he took great delight in the teaching of Greek to a class of girls, and his attitude of noble resignation, tender dignity, and resolute interest in the growing history of his race and nation is deeply impressive. He died in 1892, on June II, of a heart-complaint to which he had long been subject.

In person William Cory was short and sturdy; he was strong and vigorous; he was like the leader whom Archilochus desired, "one who is compact of frame, showing legs that bend outward, standing firm upon his feet, full of courage." He had a vigorous, massive head, with aquiline nose, and mobile lips. He was extraordinarily near-sighted, and used strong glasses, holding his book close to his eyes. He was accustomed to bewail his limited vision, as hiding from him much natural beauty, much human drama; but he observed more closely than many men of greater clearness of sight, making the most of his limited resources. He depended much upon a hearing which was preternaturally acute and sensitive, and was guided as much by the voice and manner, as by the aspect of those among whom he lived. He had a brisk, peremptory mode of address, full of humorous mannerisms of speech. He spoke and taught crisply and decisively, and uttered fine and feeling thoughts with a telling brevity. He had strong common sense, and much practical judgment.

He was intensely loyal both to institutions and friends, but never spared trenchant and luminous criticisms, and had a keen eye for weakness in any shape. He was formidable in a sense, though truly lovable; he had neither time nor inclination to make enemies, and had a generous perception of nobility of character, and of enthusiasms however dissimilar to his own. He hankered often for the wider world; he would have liked to have a hand in politics, and to have helped to make history. He often desired to play a larger part; but the very stirrings of regret only made him throw himself with intensified energy into the work of his life. He lived habitually on a higher plane than others, among the memories of great events, with a consciousness of high impersonal forces, great issues, big affairs; and yet he held on with both hands to life; he loved all that was tender and beautiful. He never lost himself in ambitious dreams or abstract speculations. He was a psychologist rather than a philosopher, and his interest and zest in life, in the relationships of simple people, the intermingling of personal emotions and happy comradeships, kept him from ever forming cynical or merely spectatorial views of humanity. He would have been far happier, indeed, if he could have practised a greater detachment; but, as it was, he gathered in, like the old warrior, a hundred spears; like Shelley he might have said—

"I fall upon the thorns of life; I bleed."

His is thus a unique personality, in its blending of intense mental energy with almost passionate emotions. Few natures can stand the strain of the excessive development of even a single faculty; and with William Cory the qualities of both heart and head were over-developed. There resulted a want of balance, of moral force; he was impetuous where he should have been calm, impulsive where he should have been discreet. But on the other hand he was possessed of an almost Spartan courage; and through sorrow and suffering, through disappointment and failure, he bore himself with a high and stately tenderness, without a touch of acrimony or peevishness. He never questioned the love or justice of God; he never raged against fate, or railed at circumstance. He gathered up the fragments with a quiet hand; he never betrayed envy or jealousy; he never deplored the fact that he had not realised his own possibilities; he suffered silently, he endured patiently.

And thus he is a deeply pathetic figure, because his great gifts and high qualities never had full scope. He might have been a great jurist, a great lawyer, a great professor, a great writer, a great administrator; and he ended as a man of erratic genius, as a teacher in a restricted sphere, though sowing, generously and prodigally, rich and fruitful seed. With great poetical force of conception, and a style both resonant and suggestive, he left a single essay of high genius, a fantastic historical work, a few books of school exercises. A privately printed volume of Letters and Journals reveals the extraordinary quality of his mind, its delicacy, its beauty, its wistfulness, its charm. There remains but the little volume of verse which is here presented, which stands apart from the poetical literature of the age. We see in these poems a singular and original contribution to the poetry of the century. The verse is in its general characteristics of the school of Tennyson, with its equable progression, its honied epithets, its soft cadences, its gentle melody. But the poems are deeply original, because they, combine a peculiar classical quality, with a frank delight in the spirit of generous boyhood. For all their wealth of idealised sentiment, they never lose sight of the fuller life of the world that waits beyond the threshold of youth, the wider issues, the glory of the battle, the hopes of the patriot, the generous visions of manhood. They are full of the romance of boyish friendships, the echoes of the river and the cricket field, the ingenuous ambitions, the chivalry, the courage of youth and health, the brilliant charm of the opening world. These things are but the prelude to, the presage of, the energies of the larger stage; his young heroes are to learn the lessons of patriotism, of manliness, of activity, of generosity, that they may display them in a wider field. Thus he wrote in "A Retrospect of School Life":—

"Much lost I; something stayed behind,
A snatch, maybe, of ancient song.
Some breathings of a deathless mind,
Some love of truth, some hate of wrong.

And to myself in games I said,
'What mean the books? can I win fame
I would be like the faithful dead,
A fearless man, and pure of blame.'"

Then, too, there are poems of a sombre yet tender philosophy, of an Epicureanism that is seldom languid, of a Stoicism that is never hard. In this world, where so much is dark, he seems to say, we must all clasp hands and move forwards, shoulder to shoulder, never forgetting the warm companionship in the presence of the blind chaotic forces that wave their shadowy wings about us. We must love what is near and dear, we must be courageous and tender-hearted in the difficult valley. The book is full of the passionate sadness of one who feels alike the intensity and the brevity of life, and who cannot conjecture why fair things must fade as surely as they bloom.

The poems then reflect a kind of Platonic agnosticism; they offer no solution of the formless mystery; but they seem rather to indicate the hope that, in the multiplying of human relationship, in devotion to all we hold dear, in the enkindling of the soul by all that is generous and noble and unselfish, lies the best hope of the individual and of the race. Uncheered by Christian hopefulness, and yet strong in their belief in the ardours and passions of humanity, these poems may help us to remember and love the best of life, its days of sunshine and youth, its generous companionships, its sweet ties of loyalty and love, its brave hopes and ardent impulses, which may be ours, if we are only loving and generous and high-hearted, to the threshold of the dark, and perhaps beyond.

ARTHUR C. BENSON.

DESIDERATO

Oh, lost and unforgotten friend,
Whose presence change and chance deny;
If angels turn your soft proud eye
To lines your cynic playmate penned,

Look on them, as you looked on me,
When both were young; when, as we went
Through crowds or forest ferns, you leant
On him who loved your staff to be;

And slouch your lazy length again
On cushions fit for aching brow
(Yours always ached, you know), and now

As dainty languishing as then,
Give them but one fastidious look,
And if you see a trace of him
Who humoured you in every whim,

Seek for his heart within his book:
For though there be enough to mark
The man's divergence from the boy,
Yet shines my faith without alloy

For him who led me through that park;
And though a stranger throw aside
Such grains of common sentiment,
Yet let your haughty head be bent

To take the jetsom of the tide;
Because this brackish turbid sea
Throws toward thee things that pleased of yore,
And though it wash thy feet no more,

Its murmurs mean: "I yearn for thee."
The world may like, for all I care,
The gentler voice, the cooler head,
That bows a rival to despair,

And cheaply compliments the dead;
That smiles at all that's coarse and rash,
Yet wins the trophies of the fight,
Unscathed, in honour's wreck and crash,

Heartless, but always in the right;.
Thanked for good counsel by the judge
Who tramples on the bleeding brave,
Thanked too by him who will not budge
From claims thrice hallowed by the grave.

Thanked, and self-pleased: ay, let him wear
What to that noble breast was due;
And I, dear passionate Teucer, dare
Go through the homeless world with you.

MIMNERMUS IN CHURCH

You promise heavens free from strife,
Pure truth, and perfect change of will;
But sweet, sweet is this human life,
So sweet, I fain would breathe it still;
Your chilly stars I can forego,
This warm kind world is all I know.

You say there is no substance here,
One great reality above:
Back from that void I shrink in fear,
And child-like hide myself in love:
Show me what angels feel. Till then,
I cling, a mere weak man, to men.

You bid me lift my mean desires
From faltering lips and fitful veins
To sexless souls, ideal quires,
Unwearied voices, wordless strains:
My mind with fonder welcome owns
One dear dead friend's remembered tones.

Forsooth the present we must give
To that which cannot pass away;
All beauteous things for which we live
By laws of time and space decay.

But oh, the very reason why
I clasp them, is because they die.

HERACLITUS

They told me, Heraclitus, they told me you were dead,
They brought me bitter news to hear and bitter tears to shed.
I wept, as I remembered, how often you and I
Had tired the sun with talking and sent him down the sky.

And now that thou art lying, my dear old Carian guest,
A handful of grey ashes, long long ago at rest,
Still are thy pleasant voices, thy nightingales, awake;
For Death, he taketh all away, but them he cannot take.

IOLE

I will not leave the smouldering pyre:
Enough remains to light again:
But who am I to dare desire
A place beside the king of men?

So burnt my dear Ochalian town;
And I an outcast gazed and groaned.
But, when my father's roof fell down,
For all that wrong sweet love atoned.

He led me trembling to the ship,
He seemed at least to love me then;
He soothed, he clasped me lip to lip:
How strange, to wed the king of men.

I linger, orphan, widow, slave,
I lived when sire and brethren died;
Oh, had I shared my mother's grave, .
Or clomb unto the hero's side!

That comrade old hath made his moan;
The centaur cowers within his den:
And I abide to guard alone
The ashes of the king of men.

Alone, beneath the night divine—
Alone, another weeps elsewhere:
Her love for him is unlike mine,
Her wail she will not let me share.

STESICHORUS

Queen of the Argives, (thus the poet spake,)
Great lady Helen, thou hast made me wise;
Veiled is the world, but all the soul awake,
Purged by thine anger, clearer far than eyes.

Peep is the darkness; for my bride is hidden,
Crown of my glory, guerdon of my song:
Preod is the vision; thou art here unbidden,
Mute and reproachful, since I did thee wrong.

Sweetest of wanderers, grievest thou for friends
Tricked by a phantom, cheated to the grave?
Woe worth the God, the mocking God, that sends
Lies to the pious, furies to the brave.

Pardon our falsehood: thou wert far away,
Gathering the lotus down the Egypt-water,
Wifely and duteous, hearing not the fray,
Taking no stain from all those years of slaughter:

Guiltless, yet mournful. Tell the poets truths;
Tell them real beauty leadeth not to strife;
Weep for the slain, those many blooming youths:
Tears such as thine might bring them back to life.

Dear, gentle lady, if the web's unthreaded,
Slander and fable fairly rent in twain,
Then, by the days when thou wert loved and wedded,
Give me, I pray, my bride's glad smile again.

The lord, who leads the Spartan host,
Stands with a little maid,
To greet a stranger from the coast
Who comes to seek his aid.

What brings the guest? a disk of brass
With curious lines engraven:
What mean the lines? stream, road, and pass,
Forest, and town, and haven.

"Lo, here Choaspes' lilied field:
Lo, here the Hermian plain:
What need we save the Doric shield
To stop the Persian's reign?

Or shall barbarians drink their nil
Upon the slopes of Tmolus?
Or trowsered robbers spoil at will
The bounties of Pactolus?

Salt lakes, burnt uplands, lie between;
The distant king moves slow;
He starts, ere Smyrna's vines are green,
Comes, when their juices flow.

Waves bright with morning smoothe thy course,
Swift row the Samian galleys;

Unconquered Colophon sounds to horse
Up the broad eastern valleys.

Is not Apollo's call enough,
The god of every Greek?
Then take our gold, and household stuff;
Claim what thou wilt, but speak."

He falters; for the waves he fears,
The roads he cannot measure;
But rates full high the gleam of spears
And dreams of yellow treasure.

He listens; he is yielding now;
Outspoke the fearless child:

"Oh, father, come away, lest thou
Be by this man beguiled."
Her lowly judgement barred the plea,
So low, it could not reach her.

The man knows more of land and sea,
But she's the truer teacher.
I mind the day, when thou didst cheat
Those rival dames with answer meet;

When, toiling at the loom,
Unblest with bracelet, ring, or chain,
Thou alone didst dare disdain
To toil in tiring-room.

Merely thou saidst: "At set of sun
My humble taskwork will be done;
And through the twilight street
Come back to view my jewels, when
Pattering through the throng of men
Go merry schoolboys' feet."

CAIUS GRACCHUS

They came, and sneered: for thou didst stand!
The web well finished up, one hand
Laid on my yielding shoulder:
The sternest stripling in the land
Grasped the other, boldly scanned
Their faces, and grew bolder:

And said: "Fair ladies, by your leave
I would exhort you spin and weave
Some frugal homely cloth.
I warn you, when I lead the tribes
Law shall strip you; threats nor bribes
Shall blunt the just man's wrath."

How strongly, gravely did he speak!
I shivered, hid my tingling cheek
Behind thy marble face;
And prayed the gods to be like him,
Firm in temper, lithe of limb,
Right worthy of our race.

Oh, mother, didst thou bear me brave?
Or was I weak, till, from the grave
So early hollowed out,
Tiberius sought me yesternight,

Blood upon his mantle white,
A vision clear of doubt?

What can I fear, oh mother, now?
His dead cold hand is on my brow;
Rest thou thereon thy lips:
His voice is in the night-wind's breath,
"Do as I did," still he saith;
With blood his finger drips.

ASTEROPE

Child of the summer cloud, upon thy birth,—
And thou art often born to die again,—
Follow loud groans, that shake the darkening earth,
And break the troublous sleep of guilty men.

Thou leapest from the thinner streams of air
To crags where vapours cling, where ocean frets;
No cave so deep, so cold, but thou art there,
Wrath in thy smile, and beauty in thy threats.

The molten sands beneath thy burning feet
Run, as thou runnest, into tubes of glass;

Old towers and trees, that proudly stood to meet
The whirlwind, let their fair invader pass.

The lone ship warring on the Indian sea
Bursts into splinters at thy sudden stroke;
Siberian mines fired long ago by thee
Still waste in helpless flame and barren smoke.

Such is thy dreadful pastime, Angel-queen,
When swooping headlong from the Armament
Thou spreadest fear along the village green,
Fear of the day when gravestones shall be rent.

And we that fear remember not, that thou,
Slewest the Theban maid, who vainly strove
To rival Juno, when the lover's vow
Was kept in wedlock by unwilling Jove.

And we forget, that when Oileus went
From the wronged virgin and the ruined fane,
When storms were howling round "Repent, Repent,"
Thy holy arrow pierced the spoiler's brain.

To perish all the proud! but chiefly he,
Who at the tramp of steeds and cymbal-beat
Proclaimed, "I thunder! Why not worship me?"
And thou didst slay him for his counterfeit.

A DIRGE

Naiad, hid beneath the bank
By the willowy river-side,
Where Narcissus gently sank,
Where unmarried Echo died,
Unto thy serene repose
Waft the stricken Anterôs.

Where the tranquil swan is borne,
Imaged in a watery glass,
Where the sprays of fresh pink thorn
Stoop to catch the boats that pass,
Where the earliest orchis grows,
Bury thou fair Anterôs.

Glide we by, with prow and oar:
Ripple shadows off the wave,
And reflected on the shore,
Haply play about the grave.
Folds of summer-light enclose
All that once was Anterôs.

On a flickering wave we gaze,
Not upon his answering eyes:
Flower and bird we scarce can praise,

Having lost his sweet replies:
Cold and mute the river flows
With our tears for Anterôs.

AN INVOCATION

I never prayed for Dryads, to haunt the woods again;
More welcome were the presence of hungering, thirst-ing men,
Whose doubts we could unravel, whose hopes we could fulfil,
Our wisdom tracing backward, the river to the rill;
Were such beloved forerunners one summer day restored,
Then, then we might discover the Muse's mystic hoard.

Oh dear divine Comatas, I would that thou and I
Beneath this broken sunlight this leisure day might lie;
Where trees from distant forests, whose names were strange to thee,
Should bend their amorous branches within thy reach to be,
And flowers thine Hellas knew not, which art hath made more fair,
Should shed their shining petals upon thy fragrant hair.

Then thou shouldst calmly listen with ever-changing looks
To songs of younger minstrels and plots of modern books,
And wonder at the daring of poets later born,
Whose thoughts are unto thy thoughts as noon-tide is to morn;
And little shouldst thou grudge them their greater strength of soul,
Thy partners in the torch-race, though nearer to the goal.

As when ancestoral portraits look gravely from the walls
Uplift youthful baron who treads their echoing halls;
And whilst he builds new turrets, the thrice ennobled heir
Would gladly wake his grandsire his home and feast to share;

So from Ægean laurels that hide thine ancient urn
I fain would call thee hither, my sweeter lore to learn.

Or in thy cedarn prison thou waitest for the bee:
Ah, leave that simple honey, and take thy food from me.
My sun is stooping westward. Entranced dreamer, haste;
There's fruitage in my garden, that I would have thee taste.
Now lift the lid a moment; now, Dorian shepherd, speak:
Two minds shall flow together, the English and the Greek.

ACADEMUS

Perhaps there's neither tear nor smile,
When once beyond the grave.
Woe's me: but let me live meanwhile
Amongst the bright and brave;

My summers lapse away beneath
Their cool Athenian shade:
And I a string for myrtle-wreath,
A whetstone unto blade;

I cheer the games I cannot play;
As stands a crippled squire
To watch his master through the fray,
Uplifted by desire.

I roam, where little pleasures fall,
As morn to morn succeeds,
To melt, or ere the sweetness pall,
Like glittering manna-beads.

The wishes dawning in the eyes,
The softly murmured thanks;
The zeal of those that miss the prize
On clamorous river-banks;

The quenchless hope, the honest choice,
The self-reliant pride,
The music of the pleading voice
That will not be denied;

The wonder flushing in the cheek,
The questions many a score,
When I grow eloquent, and speak
Of England, and of war—

Oh, better than the world of dress
And pompous dining, out,
Better than simpering and finesse
Is all this stir and rout.

I'll borrow life, and not grow old;
And nightingales and trees
Shall keep me, though the veins be cold,
As young as Sophocles.

And when I may no longer live,
They'll say, who know the truth,
He gave whatever he had to give
To freedom and to youth.

PROSPERO

Farewell, my airy pursuivants, farewell.
We part to-day, and I resign
This lonely island, and this rocky cell,
And all that hath been mine.

"Ah, whither go we? Why not follow thee,
Our human king, across the wave,
The man that rescued us from rifted tree,
Bleak marsh, and howling cave."

Oh no. The wand I wielded then is buried,
Broken, and buried in the sand.
Oh no. By mortal hands I must be ferried
Unto the Tuscan strand.

You came to cheer my exile, and to lift
The weight of silence off my lips:
With you I ruled the clouds, and ocean-drift,
Meteors, and wandering ships.

Your fancies glinting on my central mind
Fell off in beams of many hues,
Soft lambent light. Yet, severed from mankind,
Not light, but heat, I lose.

I go, before my heart be chilled. Behold,
The bark that bears me waves her flag,
To chide my loitering. Back to your mountain-hold,
And flee the tyrant hag.

Away. I hear your little voices sinking
Into the wood-notes of the breeze:
I hear you say: "Enough, enough of thinking;
Love lies beyond the seas."

AMATURUS

Somewhere beneath the sun,
These quivering heart-strings prove it,
Somewhere there must be one
Made for this soul, to move it;

Some one that hides her sweetness
From neighbours whom she slights,
Nor can attain completeness,
Nor give her heart its rights;

Some one whom I could court
With no great change of manner,
Still holding reason's fort,
Though waving fancy's banner;

A lady, not so queenly
As to disdain my hand,
Yet born to smile serenely
Like those that rule the land;

Noble, but not too proud;
With soft hair simply folded,
And bright face crescent-browed,
And throat by Muses moulded;

And eyelids lightly falling
On little glistening seas,
Deep-calm, when gales are brawling,
Though stirred by every breeze:

Swift voice, like flight of dove
Through minster arches floating,
With sudden turns, when love
Gets overnear to doting;

Keen lips, that shape soft sayings
Like crystals of the snow,
With pretty half-betrayings
Of things one may not know;

Fair hand, whose touches thrill,
Like golden rod of wonder,
Which Hermes wields at will
Spirit and flesh to sunder;

Light foot, to press the stirrup
In fearlessness and glee,
Or dance, till finches chirrup,
And stars sink to the sea.

Forth, Love, and find this maid,
Wherever she be hidden:
Speak, Love, be not afraid,
But plead as thou art bidden;

And say, that he who taught thee
His yearning want and pain,
Too dearly, dearly bought thee
To part with thee in vain.

MORTEM, QUAE VIOLAT
SUAVI A PELLIT AMOR

The plunging rocks, whose ravenous throats
The sea in wrath and mockery fills,
The smoke, that up the valley floats,
The girlhood of the growing hills;

The thunderings from the miners' ledge,
The wild assaults on nature's hoard,
The peak, that stormward bares an edge
Ground sharp in days when Titans warred;

Grim heights, by wandering clouds embraced
Where lightning's ministers conspire,
Grey glens, with tarn and streamlet laced,
Stark forgeries of primeval fire;

These scenes may gladden many a mind
Awhile from homelier thoughts released,
And here my fellow-men may find
A Sabbath and a vision-feast.

I bless them in the good they feel;
And yet I bless them with a sigh:
On me this grandeur stamps the seal
Of tyrannous mortality.

The pitiless mountain stands so sure,
The human breast so weakly heaves;
That brains decay, while rocks endure,
At this the insatiate spirit grieves.

But hither, oh ideal bride!
For whom this heart in silence aches,
Love is unwearied as the tide,
Love is perennial as the lakes;

Come thou. The spiky crags will seem
One harvest of one heavenly year,
And fear of death, like childish dream,
Will pass and flee, when thou art here.

TWO FRAGMENTS OF CHILDHOOD

When these locks were yellow as gold,
When past days were easily told,
Well I knew the voice of the sea,
Once he spake as a friend to me.

Thunder-roarings carelessly heard,
Once that poor little heart they stirred.
Why, oh, why?
Memory, Memory!
She that I wished to be with was by.

Sick was I in those misanthrope days
Of soft caresses, womanly ways;
Once that maid on the stairs I met,
Lip on brow she suddenly set.

Then flushed up my chivalrous blood
Like Swiss streams in a midsummer flood.
Then, oh, then,
Imogen, Imogen!
Hadst thou a lover, whose years were ten.

WAR MUSIC

One hour of my boyhood, one glimpse of the past,
One beam of the dawn ere the heavens were o'ercast.

I came to a castle by royalty's grace,
Forgot I was bashful, and feeble, and base.
For stepping to music I dreamt of a siege,
A vow to my mistress, a fight for my liege.
The first sound of trumpets that fell on mine ear
Set warriors around me and made me their peer.
Meseemed we were arming, the bold for the fair,
In joyous devotion and haughty despair:
The warders were waiting to draw bolt and bar,
The maidens attiring to gaze from afar:

I thought of the sally, but not the retreat,
The cause was so glorious, the dying so sweet.

I live, I am old, I return to the ground:
Blow trumpets, and still I can dream to the sound.

NUBENTI

Though the lark that upward flies
Recks not of the opening skies,
Nor discerneth grey from blue,
Nor the rain-drop from the dew:
Yet the tune which no man taught
So can quicken human thought,
That the startled fancies spring
Faster far than voice or wing.

And the songstress as she floats
Rising on her buoyant notes,
Though she may the while refuse
Homage to the nobler Muse,
Though she cannot truly tell
How her voice hath wrought the spell,
Fills the listener's eyes with tears,
Lifts him to the inner spheres.

Lark, thy morning song is done;
Overhead the silent sun
Bids thee pause. But he that heard
Such a strain must bless the bird.
Lady, thou hast hushed too soon

Sounds that cheered my weary noon;
Let met, warned by marriage bell,
Whisper, Queen of Song, farewell.

WORDS FOR A PORTUGUESE AIR

They're sleeping beneath the roses;
Oh, kiss them before they rise,
And tickle their tiny noses,
And sprinkle the dew on their eyes.
Make haste, make haste;
The fairies are caught;
Make haste.

We'll put them in silver cages,
And send them full-drest to court,
And maids of honour and pages
Shall turn the poor things to sport.
Be quick, be quick;
Be quicker than thought;
Be quick.

Their scarfs shall be pennons for lancers,
We'll tie up our flowers with their curls,
Their plumes will make fans for dancers,
Their tears shall be set with pearls.
Be wise, be wise,
Make the most of the prize;
Be wise.

They'll scatter sweet scents by winking,
With sparks from under their feet;
They'll save us the trouble of thinking,
Their voices will sound so sweet.
Oh stay, oh stay!
They're up and away;
Oh stay!

ADRIENNE AND MAURICE

(Words For The Air Commonly Called "Pestal")

I.

Fly, poor soul, fly on,
No early clouds shall stop thy roaming;
Fly, till day be gone,
Nor fold thy wings before the gloaming.
He thou lov'st will soon be far beyond thy flight,
Other lands to light,
Leaving thee in night.
Let no fear of loss thy heavenly pathway cross;
Better then to lose than now.

II.

Now, faint heart, arise,
And proudly feel that he regards thee;
Draw from godlike eyes
Some grace to last when love discards thee.
Once thou hast been blest by one too high for thee;
Fate will have him be
Great and fancy-free,

When some noble maid her hand in his hath laid,
Give him up, poor heart, and break.

THE HALLOWING OF THE FLEET

Her captains for the Baltic bound
In silent homage stood around;
Silent, whilst holy dew
Dimmed her kind eyes. She stood in tears,
For she had felt a mother's fears,
And wifely cares she knew.

She wept; she could not bear to say,
"Sail forth, my mariners, and slay
The liegemen of my foe."
Meanwhile on Russian steppe and lake
Are women weeping for the sake
Of them that seaward go.

Oh warriors, when you stain with gore,
If this indeed must be, the floor
Whereon that lady stept,
When the fierce joy of battle won
Hardens the heart of sire and son,
Remember that she wept

THE CAIRN AND THE CHURCH

A Prince went down the banks of Dee
That widen out from bleak Braemar,
To drive the deer that wander free
Amidst the pines of Lochnagar.

And stepping on beneath the birks
On the road-side he found a spot,
Which told of pibrochs, kilts, and dirks,
And wars the courtiers had forgot;

Where with the streams, as each alone
Down to the gathering river runs,
Each on one heap to cast a stone,
Came twice three hundred Farquharsons.

They raised that pile to keep for ever
The memory of the loyal clan;
Then, grudging not their vain endeavour,
Fell at Culloden to a man.

And she, whose grandsire's uncle slew
Those dwellers on the banks of Dee,
Sighed for those tender hearts and true,
And whispered: "Who would die for me?"

Oh, lady, turn thee southward. Show
Thy standard on thine own Thames-side;
Let us be called to meet thy foe,
Our Kith be pledged, our honour tried.

Now, on the stone by Albert laid,
We'll build a pile as high as theirs,
So sworn to bring our Sovereign aid,
If not with war-cries, yet with prayers.

A QUEEN'S VISIT

June 4, 1851

From vale to vale, from shore to shore,
The lady Gloriana passed,
To view her realms: the south wind bore
Her shallop to Belleisle at last.

A quiet mead, where willows bend
Above the curving wave, which rolls
On slowly crumbling banks, to send
Its hard-won spoils to lazy shoals.

Beneath an oak weird eddies play,
Where fate was writ for Saxon seer;
And yonder park is white with may,
Where shadowy hunters chased the deer.

In rows half up the chestnut, perch
Stiff-silvered fairies; busy rooks
Caw front the elm; and, rung to church,
Mute anglers drop their caddised hooks.

They troop between the dark-red walls,
When the twin towers give four-fold chimes;

And lo! the breaking groups, where falls
'Tim chequered shade of quivering limes.

'They come from field and wharf and street
With dewy hair and veined throat,
One fluor to tread with reverent feet,—
One hour of rest for ball and boat:

Like swallows gathering for their flight,
When autumn whispers, play no more,
They check the laugh, with fancies bright
Still hovering round the sacred door.

Lo! childhood swelling into seed,
Lo! manhood bursting from the bud:
Two growths, unlike; yet all agreed
To trust the movement of the blood.

They toil at games, and play with books:
They love the winner of the race,
If only he that prospers looks
On prizes with a simple grace.

The many leave the few to choose;
They scorn not him who turns aside
To woo alone a milder Muse,
If shielded by a tranquil pride.

When thought is claimed, when pain is borne,
Whate'er is done in this sweet isle,
There's none that may not lift his horn,
If only lifted with a smile.

So here dwells freedom; nor could she,
Who ruled in every clime on earth,
Find any spring more fit to be
The fountain of her festal mirth.

Elsewhere she sought for lore and art,
But hither came for vernal joy:
Nor was this all: she smote the heart
And woke the hero in the boy.

MOON-SET

Sweet moon, twice rounded in a blithe July,
Once down a wandering English stream thou leddest
My lonely boat; swans gleamed around; the sky
Throbbed overhead with meteors. Now thou sheddest
Faint radiance on a cold Arvernian plain,
Where I, far severed from that youthful crew,
Far from the gay disguise thy witcheries threw
On wave and dripping oar, still own thy reign,
Travelling with thee through many a sleepless hour.
Now shrink, like my weak will: a sterner power
Empurpleth yonder hills beneath thee piled,
Hills, where Cæsarian sovereignty was won
On high basaltic levels blood-defiled,
The Druid moonlight quenched beneath the Roman sun.

AFTER READING "MAUD"

September, 1855

Twelve years ago, if he had died,
His critic friends had surely cried:
"Death does us wrong, the fates are cross;
Nor will this age repair the loss.
Fine was the promise of his youth;
Time would have brought him deeper truth.
Some earnest of his wealth he gave,
Then hid his treasures in the grave."
And proud that they alone on earth
Perceived what might have been his worth,
They would have kept their leader's name
Linked with a fragmentary fame.
Forsooth the beech's knotless stem,
If early felled, were dear to them.

But the fair tree lives on, and spreads
Its scatheless boughs above their heads,
And they are pollarded by cares,
And give themselves religious airs,
And grow not, whilst the forest-king
Strikes high and deep from spring to spring.
So they would have his branches rise

In theoretic symmetries;
They see a twist in yonder limb,
The foliage not precisely trim;
Some gnarled roughness they lament,
Take credit for their discontent,
And count his flaws, serenely wise
With motes of pity in their eyes;
As if they could, the prudent fools,
Adjust such live-long growth to rules,
As if so strong a soul could thrive
Fixed in one shape at thirty-five.
Leave him to us, ye good and sage,
Who stiffen in your middle age.

Ye loved him once, but now forbear;
Yield him to those who hope and dare,
And have not yet to forms consigned
A rigid, ossifying mind.

One's feelings lose poetic flow
Soon after twenty-seven or so;
Professionizing moral men
Thenceforth admire what pleased them then;
The poems bought in youth they read,
And say them over like their creed.
All autumn crops of rhyme seem strange;
Their intellect resents the change.

They cannot follow to the end
Their more susceptive college-friend:
He runs from field to field, and they
Stroll in their paddocks making hay:

He's ever young, and they get old;
Poor things, they deem him over-bold:
What wonder, if they stare and scold?

A SONG

i.

Oh, earlier shall the rosebuds blow,
In after years, those happier years,
And children weep, when we lie low,
Far fewer tears, far softer tears.

ii.

Oh, true shall boyish laughter ring,
Like tinkling chimes in kinder times!
And merrier shall the maiden sing:
And I not there, and I not there.

iii.

Like lightning in the summer night
Their mirth shall be, so quick and free;
And oh! the flash of their delight
I shall not see, I may not see.

iv.

In deeper dream, with wider range,
Those eyes shall shine, but not on mine:

Unmoved, unblest, by worldly change,
The dead must rest, the dead shall rest.

A STUDY OF BOYHOOD

So young, and yet so worn with pain!
No sign of youth upon that stooping head,
Save weak half-curls, like beechen boughs that spread
With up-turned edge to catch the hurrying rain;

Such little lint-white locks, as wound
About a mother's finger long ago,
When he was blither, not more dear, for woe
Was then far off, and other sons stood round.

And she has wept since then with him
Watching together, where the ocean gave
To her child's counted breathings wave for wave,
Whilst the heart fluttered, and the eye grew dim.

And when the sun and day-breeze fell,
She kept with him the vigil of despair;
Knit hands for comfort, blended sounds of prayer,
Saw him at dawn face death, and take farewell;

Saw him grow holier through his grief,
The early grief that lined his withering brow,
As one by one her stars were quenched. And now
He that so mourned can play, though life is brief;

Not gay, but gracious; plain of speech,
And freely kindling under beauty's ray,
He dares to speak of what he loves; to-day
He talked of art, and led me on to teach,

And glanced, as poets glance, at pages
Full of bright Florence and warm Umbrian skies;
Not slighting modern greatness, for the wise
Can sort the treasures of the circling ages;

Not echoing the sickly praise,
Which boys repeat, who hear a father's guest
Prate of the London show-rooms; what is best
He firmly lights upon, as birds on sprays;

All honest, and all delicate:
No room for flattery, no smiles that ask
For tender pleasantries, no looks that mask
The genial impulses of love and hate.

Oh bards that call to bank and glen,
Ye bid me go to nature to be healed!
And lo! a purer fount is here revealed:
My lady-nature dwells in heart of men.

MERCURIALIA

Sweet eyes, that aim a level shaft
At pleasure flying from afar,
Sweet lips, just parted for a draught
Of Hebe's nectar, shall I mar
By stress of disciplinary craft
The joys that in your freedom are?

Shall the bright Queen who rules the tide
Now forward thrown, now bridled back,
Smile o'er each answering smile, then hide
Her grandeur in the transient rack,
And yield her power, and veil her pride,
And move along a ruffled track:

And shall not I give jest for jest,
Though king of fancy all the while,
Catch up your wishes half expressed,
Endure your whimsies void of guile,
Albeit with risk of such unrest
As may disturb, but not defile?

Oh, twine me myrtle round the sword,
Soft wit round wisdom over-keen:
Let me but lead my peers, no lord
With brows high arched; and lofty mien,

Set comrades round my council board
For bold debates, with jousts between.

There quiver lips, there glisten eyes,
There throb young hearts with generous hope;
Thence, playmates, rise for high emprize;
For, though he fail, yet shall ye cope
With worldling wrapped in silken lies,
With pedant, hypocrite, and pope.

REPARABO

The world will rob me of my friends,
For time with her conspires;
But they shall both to make amends
Relight my slumbering fires.

For while my comrades pass away
To bow and smirk and gloze,
Come others, for as short a stay;
And dear are these as those.

And who was this? they ask; and then
The loved and lost I praise:
"Like you they frolicked; they are men:
"Bless ye my later days."

Why fret? the hawks I trained are flown:
'Twas nature bade them range;
I could not keep their wings half-grown,
I could not bar the change.

With lattice opened wide I stand
To watch their eager flight;
With broken jesses in my hand
I muse on their delight.

And, oh! if one with sullied plume
Should droop in mid career,
My love makes signals:—"There is room,
Oh bleeding wanderer, here."

A BIRTHDAY

The graces marked the hour, when thou
Didst leave thine ante-natal rest,
Without a cry to heave a breast
Which never ached from then till now.

That vivid soul then first unsealed
Would be, they knew, a torch to wave
Within a chill and dusky cave
Whose crystals else were unrevealed.

That fine small mouth they wreathed so well
In rosy curves, would rouse to arms
A troop then bound in slumber-charms;
Such notes they gave the magic shell.

Those straying fingerlets, that clutched
At good and bad, they so did glove,
That they might pick the flowers of love,
Unscathed, from every briar they touched.

The bounteous sisters did ordain,
That thou one day with jest and whim
Should'st rain thy merriment on him
Whose life, when thou wert born, was pain.

For haply on that night they spied
A sickly student at his books,
Who having basked in loving looks
Was freezing into barren pride.

His squalid discontent they saw,
And, for that he had worshipped them
With incense and with anadem,
They willed his wintry world should thaw;

And at thy cradle did decree
That fifteen years should pass, and thou
Should'st breathe upon that pallid brow
Favonian airs of mirth and glee.

A NEW YEAR'S DAY

Our planet runs through liquid space,
And sweeps us with her in the race;
And wrinkles gather on my face,
And Hebe bloom on thine:
Our sun with his encircling spheres
Around the central sun careers;
And unto thee with mustering years
Come hopes which I resign.

'Twere sweet for me to keep thee still
Reclining halfway up the hill;
But time will not obey the will,
And onward thou must climb:
'Twere sweet to pause on this descent,
To wait for thee and pitch my tent,
But march I must with shoulders bent,
Yet farther from my prime.

I shall not tread thy battle-field,
Nor see the blazon on thy shield;
Take thou the sword I could not wield,
And leave me, and forget
Be fairer, braver, more admired;
So win what feeble hearts desired;

Then leave thine arms, when thou art tired,
To some one nobler yet.

A CRUISE

Your princely progress is begun;
And pillowed on the bounding deck
You break with dark brown hair a sun
That falls transfigured on your neck.
Sail on, and charm sun, wind, and sea.
Oh! might that love-light rest on me!

Vacantly lingering with the hours,
The sacred hours that still remain
From that rich month of fruits and flowers
Which brought you near me once again,
By thoughts of you, though roses die,
I strive to make it still July.

Soft waves are strown beneath your prow,
Like carpets for a victor's feet;
You call slow zephyrs to your brow,
In listless luxury complete:
Love, the true Halcyon, guides your ship;
Oh, might his pinion touch my lip!

I by the shrunken river stroll;
And changed, since I was left alone,
With tangled weed and rising shoal,
The loss I mourn he seems to own:

This is, how base soe'er his sloth,
This is the stream that bore us both.

For you shall granite peaks uprise
As old and scornful as your race,
And fringed with firths of lucent dyes
The jewelled beach your limbs embrace.
Oh bather, may those Western gems
Remind you of my lilied Thames.

I too have seen the castled West,
Her Cornish creeks, her Breton ports,
Her caves by knees of hermits pressed,
Her fairy islets bright with quartz:
And dearer now each well-known scene,
For what shall be than what hath been.

Obeisance of kind strangers' eyes,
Triumphant cannons' measured roar,
Doffed plumes, and martial courtesies,
Shall greet you on the Norman shore.
Oh, that I were a stranger too,
To win that first sweet glance from you.

I was a stranger once: and soon
Beyond desire, above belief,
Thy soul was as a crescent moon,
A bud expanding leaf by leaf.
I'd pray thee now to close, to wane,
So that 'twere all to do again.

A SEPARATION

I may not touch the hand I saw
So nimbly weave the violet chain;
I may not see my artist draw
That southward-sloping lawn again.
But joy brimmed over when we met,
Nor can I mourn our parting yet.

Though he lies sick and far away,
I play with those that still are here,
Not honouring him the less, for they
To me by loving him are dear:
They share, they soothe my fond regret,
Since neither they nor I forget.

His sweet strong heart so nobly beat
With scorn and pity, mirth and zeal,
That vibrant hearts of ours repeat
What they with him were wont to feel;
Still quiring in that higher key,
Till he take up the melody.

If there be any music here,
I trust it will not fail, like notes
Of May-birds, when the warning year
Abates their summer-wearied throats.

Shame on us, if we drudge once more
As dull and tuneless as before.

Without him I was weak and coarse,
My soul went droning through the hours,
His goodness stirred a latent force
That drew from others kindred powers.
Nor they nor I could think me base,
When with their prince I had found grace.

His influence crowns me, like a cloud
Steeped in the light of a lost sun:
I reign, for willing knees are bowed
And light behests are gladly done:
So Rome obeyed the lover-king,
Who drank at pure Egeria's spring.

Such honour doth my mind perplex:
For, who is this, I ask, that dares
With manhood's wounds, and virtue's wrecks,
And tangled creeds, and subtle cares,
Affront the look, or speak the name
Of one who from Elysium came.

And yet, though withered and forlorn,
I had renounced what man desires,
I'd thought some poet might be born
To string my lute with silver wires;
At least in brighter days to come
Such men as I would not lie dumb.

I saw the Sibyl's finger rest
On fate's unturned imagined page,
Believed her promise, and was blest
With dreams of that heroic age.
She sent me, ere my hope was cold,
One of the race that she foretold.

His fellows time will bring, and they,
In manifold affections free,
Shall scatter pleasures day by day
Like blossoms rained from windy tree.
So let that garden bloom; and I,
Content with one such flower, will die.

A NEW MICHONNET

The foster-child forgets his nurse:
She doth but know what he hath been,
Took him for better or for worse,
Would pet him, though he be sixteen.

He helps to weave the soft quadrille;
Ah! leave the parlour door ajar;
Those thirsting eyes shall take their fill,
And watch her darling from afar.

It is her pride to see the hand,
Which wont so wantonly to tear
Her unblanched curls, control the band,
And change the tune, with such an air.

And who so good? she thinks, or who
So fit for partners rich and tall?
Indeed she's looked the ball-room through,
And he's the loveliest lad of all.

So to her lonesome bed: and there,
If any wandering notes she hear,
She'll say in pauses of her prayer,
"He dancing still, my child! my dear!"

His gladness doth on her redound,
Though hair be grey, and eyes be dim:
At every waif of broken sound
She'll wake, and smile, and think of him.

So, noblest of the noble, go
Through regions echoing thy name;
And even on me, thy friend, shall flow
Some streamlet from thy river of fame.

Thou to the gilded youth be kind;
Shed all thy genius-rays on them;
An ancient comrade stands behind
To touch, unseen, thy mantle's hem.

A stranger to thy peers am I,
And slighted, like that poor old crone,
And yet some clinging memories try
To rate thy conquests as mine own.

Nay, when at random drops thy praise
From lips of happy lookers-on,
My tearful eyes I proudly raise,
And bid my conscious self be gone.

SAPPHICS

Love, like an island, held a single heart,
Waiting for shoreward flutterings of the breeze,
So might it waft to him that sat apart
Some angel guest from out the clouded seas.

Was it mere chance that threw within his reach
Fragments and symbols of the bliss unknown?
Was it vague hope that murmured down the beach,
Tuning the billows and the cavern's moan?

Oft through the aching void the promise thrilled:
"Thou shalt be loved, and Time shall pay his debt."
Silence returns upon the wish fulfilled,
Joy for a year, and then a sweet regret.

Idol, mine Idol, whom this touch profanes,
Pass as thou cam'st across the glimmering seas:
All, all is lost but memory's sacred pains;
Leave me, oh leave me, ere I forfeit these.

A FABLE

An eager girl, whose father buys
Some ruined thane's forsaken hall,
Explores the new domain, and tries
Before the rest to view it all.

Alone she lifts the latch, and glides
Through many a sadly curtained room,
As daylight through the doorway slides
And struggles with the muffled gloom.

With mimicries of dance she wakes
The lordly gallery's silent floor,
And climbing up on tiptoe, makes
The old-world mirror smile once more.

With tankards dry she chills her lip,
With yellowing laces veils the head,
And leaps in pride of ownership
Upon the faded marriage bed.

A harp in some dark nook she sees,
Long left a prey to heat and frost.
She smites it: can such tinklings please?
Is not all worth, all beauty, lost?

Ah! who'd have thought such sweetness clung
To loose neglected strings like those?
They answered to whate'er was sung,
And sounded as the lady chose.

Her pitying finger hurried by
Each vacant space, each slackened chord;
Nor would her wayward zeal let die
The music-spirit she restored.

The fashion quaint, the time-worn flaws,
The narrow range, the doubtful tone,
All was excused awhile, because
It seemed a creature of her own.

Perfection tires; the new in old,
The mended wrecks that need her skill,
Amuse her. If the truth be told,
She loves the triumph of her will.

With this, she dares herself persuade,
She'll be for many a month content,
Quite sure no duchess ever played
Upon a sweeter instrument.

And thus in sooth she can beguile
Girlhood's romantic hours: but soon
She yields to taste and mode and style,
A siren of the gay saloon;

And wonders how she once could like
Those drooping wires, those failing notes,

And leaves her toy for bats to strike
Amongst the cobwebs and the motes.

But enter in, thou freezing wind,
And snap the harp-strings one by one;
It was a maiden blithe and kind:
They felt her touch; their task is done.

AMAVI

Ask, mournful Muse, by one alone inspired:
What change? am I less fond, or thou less fair?
Or is it, that thy mounting soul is tired
Of duteous homage and religious care?

So many court thee that my reverent gaze
Vexes that wilful and capricious eye;
Such fine rare flatteries flow to thee, that praise,
From one whose thoughts thou know'st, seems poor
and dry.

So must it be. Thus monarchs blandly greet
Strange heralds offering tribute, and forget
The vassals ranked behind the golden seat,
Whose annual gift is counted as a debt.

Since sure of me thy liegeman once in thrall
Thou need'st not waste on me those gracious looks.
Stirred by the newborn wish to conquer all,
Leave thy first subject to his rhymes and books.

Ah! those impetuous claims that drew me forth
From my cold shadows to thy dazzling day,
Those spells that lured me to the stately North,
Those pleas against my scruples, where are they?

Oh, glorious bondage in a dreamful bower!
Oh, freedom thrice abhorred, unblest release!
Why, why hath cruel circumstance the power
To make such worship, such obedience cease?

Surely I served thee, as the wrinkled elm
Yieldeth his nature to the jocund vine,
Strength unto beauty: may the flood o'erwhelm
Root, trunk, and branch, if they have not been thine.

If thine no more, if lightly left behind,
To guard the dancing clusters thought unmeet,
It is because with gilded trellis twined
Thy liberal growth demands untempered heat.

Yet, while they spread more freely to the sun,
Those tendrils; while they wanton in the breeze
Gathering all heaven's bounties, henceforth one
Abides more honoured than the neighbouring trees.

Ah dear, there's something left of that great gift;
And humbly marvelling at thy former choice
A head once crowned with love I dare uplift,
And, for that once I pleased thee, still rejoice.

NOTES OF AN INTERVIEW

It is but little that remaineth
Of the kindness that you gave me,
And that little precious remnant you withhold.
Go free; I know that time constraineth,
Wilful blindness could not save me:
Yet you say I caused the change that I foretold.

At every sweet unasked relenting,
Though you'd tried me with caprice,
Did my welcome, did my gladness ever fail?
To-day not loud is my lamenting:
Do not chide me; it shall cease:
Could I think of vanished love without a wail?

Elsewhere, you lightly say, are blooming
All the graces I desire:
Thus you goad me to the treason of content:
If ever, when your brow is glooming,
Softer faces I admire,
Then your lightnings make me tremble and repent.

Grant this: whatever else beguileth
Restless dreaming, drowsy toil,
As a plaything, as a windfall, let me hail it.

Believe: the brightest one that smileth
To your beaming is a foil,
To the splendour breaking from you, though you veil it.

PREPARATION

Too weak am I to pray, as some have prayed,
That love might hurry straightway out of mind,
And leave an ever-vacant waste behind.

I thank thee rather, that through every grade
Of less and less affection we decline,
As month by month thy strong importunate fate
Thrusts back my claims, and draws thee toward the
great,
And shares amongst a hundred what was mine.

Proud heroes ask to perish in high noon:
I'd have refractions of the fallen day,
And heavings when the gale hath flown away,
And this slow disenchantment: since too soon,
Too surely, comes the death of my poor heart,
Be it inured to pain, in mercy, ere we part.

DETERIORA

One year I lived in high romance,
A soul ennobled by the grace
Of one whose very frowns enhance
The regal lustre of the face,
And in the magic of a smile
I dwelt as in Calypso's isle.

One year, a narrow line of blue,
With clouds both ways awhile held back:
And dull the vault that line goes through,
And frequent now the crossing rack;
And who shall pierce the upper sky,
And count the spheres? Not I, not I!

Sweet year, it was not hope you brought,
Nor after toil and storm repose,
But a fresh growth of tender thought,
And all of love my spirit knows.
You let my lifetime pause, and bade
The noontide dial cast no shade.

If fate and nature screen from me
The sovran front I bowed before,
And set the glorious creature free,
Whom I would clasp, detain, adore;

If I forego that strange delight,
Must all be lost? Not quite, not quite.

Die, little Love, without complaint,
Whom Honour standeth by to shrive:
Assoilèd from all selfish taint,
Die, Love, whom Friendship will survive.
Nor heat nor folly gave thee birth;
And briefness does but raise thy worth.

Let the grey hermit Friendship hoard
Whatever sainted Love bequeathed,
And in some hidden scroll record
The vows in pious moments breathed.
Vex not the lost with idle suit,
Oh lonely heart, be mute, be mute.

PARTING

As when a traveller, forced to journey back,
Takes coin by coin, and gravely counts them o'er,
Grudging each payment, fearing lest he lack,
Before he can regain the friendly shore;
So reckoned I your sojourn, day by day,
So grudged I every week that dropt away.

And as a prisoner, doomed and bound, upstarts
From shattered dreams of wedlock and repose,
At sudden rumblings of the market-carts,
Which bring to town the strawberry and the rose,
And wakes to meet sure death; so shuddered I,
To hear you meditate your gay Good-bye.

But why not gay? For, if there's aught you lose,
It is but drawing off a wrinkled glove
To turn the keys of treasuries, free to choose
Throughout the hundred-chambered house of love,
This pathos draws from you, though true and kind,
Only bland pity for the left-behind.

We part; you comfort one bereaved, unmanned;
You calmly chide the silence and the grief;
You touch me once with light and courteous hand,
And with a sense of something like relief

You turn away from what may seem to be
Too hard a trial of your charity.

So closes in the life of life; so ends
The soaring of the spirit. What remains?
To take whate'er the Muse's mother lends,
One sweet sad thought in many soft refrains
And half reveal in Coan gauze of rhyme
A cherished image of your joyous prime.

ALL THAT WAS POSSIBLE

Slope under slope the pastures dip
With ribboned waterfalls, and make
Scant room for just a village strip,
The setting of a sapphire lake.

And here, when summer draws the kine
To upland grasses patched with snow,
Our travellers rest not, only dine,
Then driven by Furies, onward go.

For pilgrims of the pointed stick,
With passport case for scallop shell,
Scramble for worshipped Alps too quick
To care for vales where mortals dwell.

Twice daily swarms the hostel's pier,
Twice daily is the table laid;
And, "Oh, that some would tarry here!"
Sighs Madeline, the serving-maid.

She shows them silly carven stuff;
Some sneer, but others smile and buy;
And these light smiles are quite enough
To make the wistful maiden sigh.

She scans the face, but not the mind;
She learns their taste in wines and toys,
But, seem they thoughtful and refined,
She fain would know their cares, their joys.

For man is not as horse and hound,
Who turn to meet their lord's caress,
Yet never miss the touch or sound,
When absence brings unconsciousness.

Not such the souls that can reflect;
Too mild they may be to repine;
But sometimes, winged with intellect,
They strain to pass the bounding line.

And to have learnt our pleasant tongue
In English mansions, gave a sense
Of something bitter-sweet, that stung
The pensive maiden of Brientz.

I will not say she wished for aught;
For, failing guests, she duly spun,
And saved for marriage; but one thought
Would still in alien channels run.

And when at last a lady came,
Not lovely, but with twofold grace,
For courtly France had tuned her name,
Whilst England reigned in hair and face;

And illness bound her many a day,
A willing captive, to the mere,

In peace, though home was far away,
For Madeline's talking brought it near.

Then delicate words unused before
Rose to her lips, as amber shines
Thrown by the wave upon the shore
From unimagined ocean-mines;

And then perceptions multiplied,
Foreshadowings of the heart came true,
And interlaced on every side
Old girlish fancies bloomed and grew;

And looks of higher meaning gleamed
Like azure sheen of mountain ice,
And common household service seemed
The wageless work of Paradise.

But autumn downward drove the kine,
And clothed the wheel with flaxen thread,
And sprinkled snow upon the pine,
And bowed the silent spinster's head.

Then Europe's tumult scared the spring,
And checked the Northern travel-drift:
Yet to Brientz did summer bring
An English letter and a gift;

And Madeline took them with a tear:
"How gracious to remember me!
Her words I'll keep from year to year,
Her face in heaven I hope to see."

SCHEVENINGEN AVENUE

Oh, that the road were longer,
A mile, or two, or three!
So might the thought grow stronger
That flows from touch of thee.

Oh little slumbering maid,
If thou wert five years older,
Thine head would not be laid
So simply on my shoulder!

Oh, would that I were younger,
Oh, were I more like thee,
I should not faintly hunger
For love that cannot be.

A girl might be caressed,
Beside me freely sitting;
A child on me might rest,
And not like thee, unwitting.

Such honour is thy mother's
Who smileth on thy sleep,
Or for the nurse who smothers
Thy cheek in kisses deep.

And but for parting day,
And but for forest shady,
From me they'd take away
The burden of their lady.

Ah thus to feel thee leaning
Above the nursemaid's hand,
Is like a stranger's gleaning,
Where rich men own the land;

Chance gains, and humble thrift,
With shyness much like thieving,
No notice with the gift,
No thanks with the receiving.

Oh peasant, when thou starvest
Outside the fair domain,
Imagine there's a harvest
In every treasured grain.

Make with thy thoughts high cheer,
Say grace for others dining,
And keep thy pittance clear
From poison of repining.

1859.

MELLIREN

Can you so fair and young forecast
The sure, the cruel day of doom;
Must I believe that you at last
Will fall, fall, fall down to the tomb?
Unclouded, fearless, gentle soul,
You greet the foe whose threats you hear;
Your lifted eyes discern the goal,
Your blood declares it is not near.

Feel deeply; toil through weal and woe,
Love England, love a friend, a bride.
Bid wisdom grow, let sorrow flow,
Make many weep when you have died.
When you shall die—what seasons lie
'Twixt that great Then and this sweet Now!
What blooms of courage for that eye,
What thorns of honour for that brow!

Oh mortal, too dear to me, tell me thy choice,
Say how wouldst thou die, and in dying rejoice?

Will you perish, calmly sinking
To a sunless deep sea cave,
Folding hands, and kindly thinking
Of the friend you tried to save?

Will you let your sweet breath pass
On the arms of children bending,
Gazing on the sea of glass,
Where the lovelight has no ending?

Or in victory stern and fateful,
Colours wrapt round shattered breast,
English maidens rescued, grateful,
Whispering near you, "Conqueror, rest;"
Or an old tune played once more,
Tender cadence oft repeated,
Moonlight shed through open door,
Angel wife beside you seated.

Whatever thy death may be, child of my heart,
Long, long shall they mourn thee that see thee depart.

1860

A MERRY PARTING

With half a moon, and cloudlets pink,
And water-lilies just in bud,
With iris on the river brink,
And white weed garlands on the mud,
And roses thin and pale as dreams,
And happy cygnets born in May,
No wonder if our country seems
Drest out for Freedom's natal day.

We keep the day; but who can brood
On memories of unkingly John,
Or of the leek His Highness chewed,
Or of the stone he wrote upon?
To Freedom born so long ago,
We do devoir in very deed,
If heedless as the clouds we row
With fruit and wine to Runnymede.

Ah! life is short, and learning long;
We're midway through our mirthful June,
And feel about for words of song
To help us through some dear old tune.
We firmly, fondly seize the joy,
As tight as fingers press the oar,

With love and laughter girl and boy
Hold the sweet days, and make them more.

And when our northern stars have set
For ever on the maid we lose,
Beneath our feet she'll not forget
How speed the hours with Eton crews.
Then round the world, good river, run,
And though with you no boat may glide,
Kind river, bear some drift of fun
And friendship to the exile bride.

June 15th, 1861.

SCHOOL FENCIBLES

We come in arms, we stand ten score,
Embattled on the castle green;
We grasp our firelocks tight, for war
Is threatening, and we see our Queen.

And "will the churls last out till we
Have duly hardened bones and thews
For scouring leagues of swamp and sea
Of braggart mobs and corsair crews?

We ask; we fear not scoff or smile
At meek attire of blue and grey,
For the proud wrath that thrills our isle
Gives faith and force to this array.

So great a charm is England's right,
That hearts enlarged together flow,
And each man rises up a knight
To work the evil-thinkers woe.

And, girt with ancient truth and grace,
We do our service and our suit,
And each can be, what'er his race,
A Chandos or a Montacute.

Thou, Mistress, whom we serve to-day,
Bless the real swords that we shall wield,
Repeat the call we now obey
In sunset lands, on some fair field.

Thy flag shall make some Huron Rock
As dear to us as Windsor's keep,
And arms thy Thames hath nerved shall mock
The surgings of th' Ontarian deep.

The stately music of thy Guards,
Which times our march beneath thy ken,
Shall sound, with spells of sacred bards,
From heart to heart, when we are men.

And when we bleed on alien earth,
We'll call to mind how cheers of ours
Proclaimed a loud uncourtly mirth
Amongst thy glowing orange bowers.

And if for England's sake we fall,
So be it, so thy cross be won,
Fixed by kind hands on silvered pall,
And worn in death, for duty done.

Ah! thus we fondle Death, the soldier's mate,
Blending his image with the hopes of youth
To hallow all; meanwhile the hidden fate
Chills not our fancies with the iron truth.

Death from afar we call, and Death is here,
To choose out him who wears the loftiest mien;

And Grief, the cruel lord who knows no peer,
Breaks through the shield of love to pierce our
Queen.

1861.

BOCONNOC

Who so distraught could ramble here,
From gentle beech to simple gorse,
From glen to moor, nor cease to fear
The world's impetuous bigot force,
Which drives the young before they will,
And when they will not drives them still.

Come hither, thou that would'st forget
The gamester's smile, the trader's vaunt,
The statesman actor's face hard set,
The kennel cry that cheers his taunt,
Come where pure winds and rills combine
To murmur peace round virtue's shrine.

Virtue—men thrust her back, when these
Rode down for Charles and right divine,
And those with dogma Genevese
Restored in faith their wavering line.
No virtue in religious camps,
No heathen oil in Gideon's lamps.

And now, when forcing seasons bud
With prophet, hero, saint, and quack,
When creeds and fashions heat the blood,
And transcendental tonguelets clack,

Sweet Virtue's lyre we hardly know,
And think her odes quite rococo.

Well, be it Roman, be it worse,
When Pelhams reigned in George's name
Poets were safe from sneer or curse
Who gave a patriot classic fame,
And goodness, void of passion, knit
The hearts of Lyttelton and Pitt.

That age was as a neutral vale
'Twixt uplands of tumultuous strife,
And turning from the sects to hail
Composure and a graceful life,
Here, where the fern-clad streamlet flows,
Boconnoc's guests ensured repose.

That charm remains; and he who knows
The root and stock of freedom's laws,
Unscared by frenzied nations' throes,
And hugging yet the good old cause,
Finds in the shade these beeches cast
The wit, the fragrance of the past.

Octave of St. Bartholomew, 1862.

A SKETCH AFTER BRANTÔME

The door hath closed behind the sighing priest,
The last absolving Latin duly said,
And night, barred slowly backward from the East,
Lets in the dawn to mock a sleepless bed;

The bed of one who yester even took
From scented aumbries store of silk and lace,
From caskets beads and rings, for one last look,
One look, which left the teardrops on her face;

A lady, who hath loved the world, the court,
Loved youth and splendour, loved her own sweet
soul,
And meekly stoops to learn that life is short,
Dame Nature's pitiful gift, a beggar's dole.

Sweet life, ah! let her live what yet remains.
Call, quickly call, the page who bears the lute;
Bid him attune to descant of sad strains
The lily voice we thought for ever mute.

The sorrowing minstrel at the casement stands
And bends before the sun that gilds his wires,
And prays a blessing on his faltering hands,
That they may serve his lady's last desires.

"Play something old and soft, a song I knew;
Play *La défaite des Suisses,*" Then pearly notes
Come dropping one by one, and with the dew
Down on the breath of morning music floats.

He played as far as *tout est perdu* and wept.
"*Tout est perdu* again, once more," she sighed;
And on, still softer on, the music crept,
And softly, at the pause, the listener died.

1862.

ON LIVERMEAD SANDS

For waste of scheme and toil we grieve,
For snowflakes on the wave we sigh,
For writings on the sand that leave
Naught for to-morrow's passer-by.

Waste, waste; each knoweth his own worth,
And would be something ere he sink
To silence, ere he mix with earth,
And part with love, and cease to think.

Shall I then comfort thee and me,
My neighbour, preaching thus of waste?
Count yonder planet fragments; see,
The meteors into darkness haste.

Lo! myriad germs at random float,
Fall on no fostering home, and die
Back to mere elements; every mote
Was framed for life as thou, as I.

For ages over soulless eyes,
Ere man was born, the heavens in vain
Dipt clouds in dawn and sunset dyes
Unheeded, and shall we complain?

Aye, Nature plays that wanton game
And Nature's hierophants may smile,
Contented with their lore; no blame
To rhymers if they groan meanwhile.

Since that which yearns towards minds of men,
Which flashes down from brain to lip,
Finds but cold truth in mammoth den,
With spores, with stars, no fellowship.

Say we that our ungarnered thought
Drifts on the stream of all men's fate,
Our travail is a thing of naught,
Only because mankind is great.

Born to be wasted, even so,
And doomed to feel, and lift no voice;
Yet not unblessed, because I know
So many other souls rejoice.

1863.

LACORDAIRE AT OXFORD

Lost to the Church and deaf to me, this town
Yet wears a reverend garniture of peace.
Set in a land of trade, like Gideon's fleece
Bedewed where all is dry; the Pope may frown;
But, if this city is the shrine of youth,
How shall the Preacher lord of virgin souls,
When by glad streams and laughing lawns he strolls,
How can he bless them not? Yet in sad sooth,
When I would love these English gownsmen, sighs
Heave my frail breast, and weakness dims mine eyes.

These strangers heed me not. Far off in France
Are young men not so fair, and not so cold,
My listeners. Were they here, their greeting glance
Might charm me to forget that I were old.

1863.

A RETROSPECT OF SCHOOL LIFE

I go, and men who know me not,
When I am reckoned man, will ask,
"What is it then that thou hast got
By drudging through that five-year task?

"What knowledge or what art is thine?
Set out thy stock, thy craft declare."
Then this child-answer shall be mine,
"I only know they loved me there."

There courteous strivings with my peers,
And duties not bound up in books,
And courage fanned by stormy cheers,
And wisdom writ in pleasant looks,

And hardship buoyed with hope, and pain
Encountered for the common weal,
And glories void of vulgar gain,
Were mine to take, were mine to feel.

Nor from Apollo did I shrink
Like Titans chained; but sweet and low
Whispered the Nymphs, who seldom think:
"Up, up for action, run and row!"

He let me, though his smile was grave,
Seek an Egeria out of town
Beneath the chestnuts; he forgave;
And should the jealous Muses frown?

Fieldward some remnants of their lore
Went with me, as the rhymes of Gray
Annealed the heart of Wolfe for war
When drifting on his starlit way.

Much lost I; something stayed behind,
A snatch, maybe, of ancient song;
Some breathings of a deathless mind,
Some love of truth, some hate of wrong.

And to myself in games I said,
"What mean the books? Can I win fame?
I would be like the faithful dead
A fearless man, and pure of blame.

I may have failed, my School may fail;
I tremble, but thus much I dare;
I love her. Let the critics rail,
My brethren and my home are there.

July 28th, 1863.

CLOVELLY BEACH

Oh, music! breathe me something old to-day,
Some fine air gliding in from far away,
Through to the soul that lies behind the clay.

This hour, if thou did'st ever speak before,
Speak in the wave that sobs upon the shore,
Speak in the rill that trickles from the moor.

Known was this sea's slow chant when I was young;
To me these rivulets sing as once they sung,
No need this hour of human throat and tongue.

The Dead who loved me heard this selfsame tide.
Oh that the Dead were listening by my side,
And I could give the fondness then denied.

Once in the parlour of my mother's sire
One sang, "And ye shall walk in silk attire."
Then my cold childhood woke to strange desire.

That was an unconfessed and idle spell,
A drop of dew that on a blossom fell;
And what it wrought I cannot surely tell.

Far off that thought and changed, like lines that stay
On withered canvas, pink and pearly grey,
When rose and violet hues have passed away.

Oh, had I dwelt with music since that night!
What life but that is life, what other flight
Escapes the plaguing doubts of wrong and right!

Oh music! once I felt the touch of thee,
Once when this soul was as the chainless sea.
Oh, could'st thou bid me even now be free!

April, 1865.

AN EPOCH IN A SWEET LIFE

This sun, whose javelins strike and gild the wheat,
Who gives the nectarine half an orb of bloom,
Burns on my life no less, and beat by beat
Shapes that grave hour when boyhood hears her doom.

Between this glow of pious eve and me,
Lost moments, thick as clouds of summer flies,
Specks of old time, which else one could not see,
Made manifest in the windless calm, arise.

Streaks fairy green are traced on backward ways,
Through vacant regions lightly overleapt,
With pauses, where in soft pathetic haze
Are phantoms of the joys that died unwept.

Seven years since one, who bore with me the yoke
Of household schooling, missed me from her side.
When called away from sorrowing woman folk
A prouder task with brothers twain I plied.

I came a child, and home was round me still,
No terror snapt the silken cord of trust;
My accents changed not, and the low "I will"
Silenced like halcyon plumes the loud "you must."

I lisped my Latin underneath the gloom
Of timbers dark as frowning usher's looks,
Where thought would stray beyond that sordid room
To saucy chessmen and to feathered hooks.

And soon I sat below my grandsire's bust,
Which in the school he loved not deigns to stand,
That Earl, who forced his compeers to be just,
And wrought in brave old age what youth had planned.

But no ancestral majesties could fix
The wistful eye, which fell, and fondly read,
Fresh carven on the panel, letters six,
A brother's name, more sacred than the dead.

How far too sweet for school he seemed to me,
How ripe for combat with the wits of men,
How childlike in his manhood! Can it be?
Can I indeed be now what he was then?

He past from sight; my laughing life remained
Like merry waves that ripple to the bank,
Curved round the spot where longing eyes are strained,
Because beneath the lake a treasure sank.

Dear as the token of a loss to some,
And praised for likeness, this was well; and yet
'Twas better still that younger friends should come,
Whose love might grow entwined with no regret.

They came; and one was of a northern race,
Who bore the island galley on his shield,

Grand histories on his name, and in his face
A bright soul's ardour fearlessly revealed.

We trifled, toiled, and feasted, far apart
From churls, who wondered what our friendship meant;
And in that coy retirement heart to heart
Drew closer, and our natures were content.

My noblest playmate lost, I still withdrew
From dull excitement which the Graces dread,
And talked in saunterings with the gentle few
Of tunes we practised, and of rhymes we read.

We swam through twilight waters, or we played
Like spellbound captives in the Naiad's grot;
Coquetted with the oar, and wooed the shade
On dainty banks of shy forget-me-not.

Oh Thames! my memories bloom with all thy flowers,
Thy kindness sighs to me from every tree:
Farewell I I thank thee for the frolic hours,
I bid thee, whilst thou flowest, speak of me.

July 28th, 1864.

PHAEDRA'S NURSE

A plague on the whimsies of sickly folk!
What am I to do? What not?
Why, here's the fair sky, and here you lie
With your couch in a sunny spot.
For this you were puling whenever you spoke,
Craving to lie outside,
And now you'll be sure not to bide.

You won't lie still for an hour;
You'll want to be back to your bower—
Longing, and never enjoying,
Shifting from yea to nay.
For all that you taste is cloying,
And sweet is the far away.

'Tis hard to be sick, but worse
To have to sit by and nurse,
For that is single, but this is double,
The mind in pain, and the hands in trouble.
The life men live is a weary coil,
There is no rest from woe and toil;
And if there's aught elsewhere more dear
Than drawing breath as we do here,
That darkness holds
In black inextricable folds.

Lovesick it seems are we
Of this, whate'er it be,
That gleams upon the earth;
Because that second birth,
That other life no man hath tried.

What lies below
No god will show,
And we to whom the truth's denied
Drift upon idle fables to and fro.

BELOW BOULTER'S LOCK

The aspen grows on the maiden's bank,
Down swoops the breeze on the bough,
Quick rose the gust, and suddenly sank,
Like wrath on my sweetheart's brow.

The tree is caught, the boat dreads nought,
Sheltered and safe below;
The bank is high, and the wind runs by,
Giving us leave to row.

The bank was dipping low and lower,
Showing the glowing west,
The oar went slower, for either rower
The river was heaving her breast.

That sunset seemed to my dauntless steerer
The lifting and breaking of day,
That flush on the wave to me was dearer
Than shade on a windless way.

June 2nd, 1868.

FROM HALS DON TO CHELTENHAM TO TWO LITTLE LADIES.

Across three shires I stretch and lean,
To gaze beyond the hills that screen
The trustful eyes and gracious mien
Of unforgotten Geraldine.

Up Severn sea my fancy leadeth,
And past the springs of Thames it speedeth,
On to the brilliant town, which needeth,
Far less than I, the laugh of Edith.

Sad gales have changed my woodland scene
To russet-brown from gold and green;
Cold and forlorn like me hath been
The boat that carried Geraldine.

On silent paths the whistler weedeth,
And what his tune is no one heedeth;
On hay beneath the linhay feedeth
The ass that felt the hand of Edith.

Oh cherished thought of Geraldine,
I'd rhyme till summer, if the Queen
Would blow her trumpets and proclaim
Fresh rhymes for that heroic name.

Oh babbler gay as river stickle,
Next year you'll be too old to tickle;
But while my Torridge flows I'll say
"Blithe Edith liked me half day."

A POOR FRENCH SAILOR'S
SCOTTISH SWEETHEART

I cannot forget my jo,
I bid him be mine in sleep;
But battle and woe have changed him so,
There's nothing to do but weep.

My mother rebukes me yet,
And I never was meek before;
His jacket is wet, his lip cold set,
He'll trouble our home no more.

Oh breaker of reeds that bend!
Oh quencher of tow that smokes!
I'd rather descend to my sailor friend
Than prosper with lofty folks.

I'm lying beside the gowan,
My jo in the English bay;
I'm Annie Rowan, his Annie Rowan,
He called me his *bien-aimée*.

I'll hearken to all you quote,
Though I'd rather be deaf and free;
The little he wrote in the sinking boat
Is Bible and charm for me.

A GARDEN GIRL

Oh, scanty white garment! they ask why I wear you,
Such thin chilly vesture for one that is frail,
And dull words of prose cannot truly declare you
To be what I bid you be, love's coat of mail.

You were but a symbol of cleanness and rest,
To don in the summer time, three years ago;
And now you encompass a care-stricken breast
With fabric of fancy to keep it aglow.

For when it was Lammastide two before this,
When freshening my face after freshening my lilies,
A door opened quickly, and down fell a kiss,
The lips unforeseen were my passionate Willie's.

My Willie was travel-worn, Willie was cold,
And I might not keep but a dear lock of hair.
I clad him in silk and I decked him with gold,
But welcome and fondness were choked in despair.

I follow the wheels, and he turns with a sob,
We fold our mute hands on the death of the hour;
For heart-breaking virtues and destinies rob
The soul of her nursling, the thorn of her flower.

The lad's mind is rooted, his passion red-fruited,
The head I caressed is another's delight;
And I, though I stray through the year sorrow-suited,
At Lammas, for Willie's sake, robe me in white.

TO TWO YOUNG LADIES

There are, I've read, two troops of years,
One troop is called the teens;
They bring sweet gifts to little dears,
Ediths and Geraldines.

The others have no certain name,
Though children of the sun,
They come to wrinkled men, and claim
Their treasures one by one.

There is a hermit faint and dry,
In things called rhymes he dabbles,
And seventeen months have heard him sigh
For Cissy and for Babbles.

Once, when he seemed to be bedridden,
These girls said, "Make us lines,"
He tried to court, as he was bidden,
His vanished Valentines.

Now, three days late, yet ere they ask,
He's meekly undertaken
To do his sentimental task,
Philandering, though forsaken.

I pace my paradise, and long
To show it off to Peris;
They come not, but it can't be wrong
To raise their ghosts by queries.

Is Geraldine in flowing robes?
Has Edith rippling curls?
And do their ears prolong the lobes
Weighed down with gold and pearls?

And do they know the verbs of France?
And do they play duetts?
And do they blush when led to dance?
And are they called coquettes?

Oh, Cissy, if the heartless year
Sets our brief loves asunder!
Oh, Babbles, whom I daren't call dear!
What can I do but wonder?

I wonder what you're both become,
Whether you're children still;
I pause with fingers twain and thumb
Closed on my faltering quill;

I pause to think how I decay,
And you win grace from Time.
Perhaps ill-natured folks would say
He's pausing for a rhyme.

The sun, who drew us far apart,
Might lessen my regrets,

Would he but deign to use his art
In painting your vignettes.

Then though I groaned for losing half
Of joys that memory traces,
I could forego the talk, the laugh,
In welcoming the faces.

A HOUSE AND A GIRL

The strawberry tree and the crimson thorn,
And Fanny's myrtle and William's vine,
And honey of bountiful jessamine,
Are gone from the homestead where I was born.

I gaze from my Grandfather's terrace wall,
And then I bethink me how once I stept
Through rooms where my Mother had blest me, and wept
To yield them to strangers, and part with them all.

My Father, like Matthew the publican, ceased
Full early from hoarding with stainless mind,
To Torrington only and home inclined,
Where brotherhood, cousinhood, graced his feast.

I meet his remembrance in market lane,
'Neath town-hall pillars and churchyard limes,
In streets where he tried a thousand times
To chasten anger and soften pain.

Ah I would there were some one that I could aid,
Though lacking the simpleness, lacking the worth,
Yet wanted and trusted by right of birth,
Some townfellow stripling, some Torrington maid.

Oh pitiful waste! oh stubborn neglect!
Oh pieties smothered for thirty years!
Oh gleanings of kindness in dreams and tears!
Oh drift cast up from a manhood wrecked!

There's one merry maiden hath carelessly crossed
The threshold I dread, and she never discerns
In keepsakes she thanks me for, lessons she learns,
A sign of the grace that I squandered and lost.

My birthplace to Meg is but window and stone,
My knowledge a wilderness where she can stray,
To keep what she gathers or throw it away;
So Meg lets me laugh with her, mourning alone.

A FELLOW PASSENGER UNKNOWN

Maiden, hastening to be wise,
Maiden, reading with a rage,
Envy fluttereth round the page
Whereupon thy downward eyes
Rove and rest, and melt maybe—
Virgin eyes one may not see,
Gathering as the bee
Takes from cherry tree;
As the robin's bill
Frets the window sill,
Maiden, bird, and bee,
Three from me half hid,
Doing what we did
When our minds were free.

Those romantic pages wist
What romance is in the look.
Oh, that I could be so bold,
So romantic as to bold
Half an hour the pensive wrist,
And the burden of the book.

NUREMBERG CEMETERY

Outside quaint Albert Durer's town,
Where Freedom set her stony crown,
Whereof the gables red and brown
Curve over peaceful forts that screen
Spring bloom and garden lanes between
The scarp and counter-scarp. Her feet
One highday of Saint Paraclete
Were led along the dolorous street
By stepping stones towards love and heaven
And pauses of the soul twice seven.

Beneath the flowerless trees, where May,
Proud of her orchards' fine array,
Abates her claim and holds no sway,
Past iron tombs, the useless shields
Of cousins slain in Elsass fields,
The girl, with fair neck meekly bowed.

Mores bravely through a sauntering crowd,
Hastening, as she was bid, to breathe
Above the breathless, and enwreathe,
With pansies earned by spinster thrift,
And lillybells, a wooer's gift,
A stone which glimmers in the shade
Of yonder silent colonnade,

Over against the slates that hold
Marie in lines of slender gold,
A token wrought by fictive fingers,
A garland, last year's offering, lingers,
Hung out of reach, and facing north.
And lo! thereout a wren flies forth,
And Gertrude, straining on toetips,
Just touches with her prayerful lips
The warm home which a bird unskilled
In grief and hope knows how to build.

The maid can mourn, but not the wren.
Birds die, death's shade belongs to men.

1877.

MORTAL THING NOT WHOLLY CLAY

J'aurai passé sur la terre,
N'ayant rien aimé que l'amour.

Mortal thing not wholly clay,
Mellowing only to decay,
Speak, for airs of spring unfold
Wistful sorrows long untold.

Under a poplar turning green,
Say for age that seems so bold,
Oh, the saddest words to say,
"This might have been."

Twenty, thirty years ago—
Woe, woe, the seasons flow—
Beatings of a zephyr's plume
Might have broken down the doom.

Gossamer scruples fell between
Thee and this that might have been;
Now the clinging cobwebs grow;
Ah! the saddest loss is this,
A good maid's kiss.

Soon, full soon, they will be here,
Twisting withies for the bier;
Under a heathen yew-tree's shade
Will a wasted heart be laid—
Heart that never dared be dear.

Leave it so, to lie unblest,
Priest of love, just half confessed.

A SICK FRENCH POET'S
ENGLISH FRIENDS

When apple buds began to swell,
And Procne called for Philomel,
Down there, where Seine caresseth sea
Two lassies deigned, or chanced, to be
Playmates or votaries for me,
Miss Euphrasie, Miss Eulalie.

Then dates of birth dropt out of mind,
For one was brave as two were kind;
In cheerful vigil one designed
A maze of wit for two to wind;
And that grey Muse who served the three
Broke daylight into reverie.

Peace lit upon a fluttering vein,
And, self forgetting, on the brain,
On rifts, by passion wrought, again
Splashed from the sky of childhood rain;
And rid of afterthought were we,
And from foreboding sweetly free.

Now falls the apple, bleeds the vine,
And moved by some autumnal sign,
I, who in spring was glad, repine,

And ache without my anodyne.
Oh things that were, oh things that are,
Oh setting of my double star!

This day this way an Iris came,
And brought a scroll, and showed a name.
Now surely they who thus reclaim
Acquaintance should relight a flame.
So speed, gay steed, that I may see
Dear Euphrasie, dear Eulalie.

Behind this ivy screen are they
Whose girlhood flowered on me last May.
The world is lord of all; I pray
They be not courtly—who can say?
Well, well, remembrance held in fee
Is good, nay, best. I turn and flee.

L'OISEAU BLEU

Down with the oar, I toil no more.
Trust to the boat; we rest, we float.
Under the loosestrife and alder we roam
To seek and search for the halcyon's home.

Blue bird, pause; thou hast no cause
To grudge me the sight of fishbones white.
Thine is the only nest now to find.
Show it me, birdie; be calm, be kind.

Wander all day in quest of prey,
Dart and gleam, and ruffle the stream;
Then for the truth that the old folks sing,
Comfort the twilight, and droop thy wing.

HOME, PUP!

Euphemia Seton of Urchinhope,
The wife of the farmer of Tynnerandoon,
Stands lifting her eyes to the whitening slope,
And longs for her laddies at suppertime soon.

The laddies, the dog, and the witless sheep,
Are bound to come home, for the snow will be deep.
The mother is pickling a scornful word
To throw at the head of the elder lad, Hugh;
But talkative Jamie, as gay as a bird,
Will have nothing beaten save snow from his shoe.
He has fire in his eyes, he has curls on his head,
And a silver brooch and a kerchief red.

Poor Hugh, trudging on with his collie pup Jess,
Has kept his plain mind to himself all the way,
Just quietly giving his dog the caress
Which no one gave him for a year and a day.
And luckily quadrupeds seldom despise
Our lumbering wits and our lack-lustre eyes.

Deep down in the corrie, high up on the brae,
Where Shinnel and Scar tumble down from the rock
The wicked white ladies have been at their play,
The wind has been pushing the leewardly flock.

The white land should tell where the creatures are gone,
But snow hides the snow that their hooves have been on.

Ah! down there in Urchinhope nobody knows
How blinding the flakes, and the north wind how cruel.
Euphemia's gudeman will come for his brose,
But far up the hill is her darling, her jewel.
She sees something crimson. "Oh, gudeman, look up!
There's Jamie's cravat on the neck of the pup."

"Where, where have ye been, Jess, and where did ye leave him?
Now just get a bite, pup, then show me my pet.
Poor Jamie 'll be tired, and the sleep will deceive him;
Oh, stir him, oh, guide him, before the sun set!"
"Quick, Jock, bring a lantern! quick, Sandie, some wraps!
Before ye win till him 'twill darken, perhaps."

Jess whimpered; the young moon was down in the west;
A shelter-stone jutted from under the hill;
Stiff hands beneath Jamie's blue bonnet were pressed,
And over his beating heart one that was still.
Bareheaded and coatless, to windward lay Hugh,
And high on his back the snow gathered and grew.

"Now fold them in plaids, they'll be up with the sun;
Their bed will be warm, and the blood is so strong.
How wise to send Jessie; now cannily run.
Poor pup, are ye tired? we'll be home before long."
Jess licked a cold cheek, and the bonny boy spoke:
"Where's Hugh?" The pup whimpered, but Hugh never woke.

A SOLDIER'S MIRACLE

'Twas when we learnt we could be beat;
Our star misled us, and' we strayed.
Elsewhere the host was in retreat;
We were a guideless lost brigade.

We stumbled on a town in doubt,
To halt and sup we were full fain,
The man that held the chart cried out,
"'Tis Vaucouleurs in old Lorraine."

In Vaucouleurs we will not doubt,
For here, when need was sore, Saint Jane
Arose, and girt herself to rout
The foes that troubled her Lorraine.

So here we feast in faith to-night,
To-morrow we'll rejoin the host
Drink, drink! the wine is pure and bright,
And Jane our maiden is the toast.

But I, that faced the window, caught
A passing cloud, a foreign plume,
A Prussian helmet; and the thought
Of peril chilled the tavern room.

We rose, we glared through twilight panes,
We muttered curses bosom-deep;
A tell-tale gallop scared the lanes,
We grudged to spoil our comrades' sleep.

Then louder than the Uhlan's hoof
Fell storm from sky and flood on banks,
September's passion smote the roof;
We blest it, and to Jane gave thanks.

Betwixt us and that Uhlan's mates
A bridgless river strongly flowed.
A sign was shown that checked the fates,
And on that storm our maiden rode.

A BALLAD FOR A BOY

When George the Third was reigning a hundred years ago,
He ordered Captain Farmer to chase the foreign foe.
"You're not afraid of shot," said he, "you're not afraid of wreck,
So cruise about the west of France in the frigate called *Quebec*.

Quebec was once a Frenchman's town, but twenty years ago
King George the Second sent a man called General Wolfe, you know,
To clamber up a precipice and look into Quebec,
As you'd look down a hatchway when standing on the deck.

If Wolfe could beat the Frenchmen then so you can beat them now.
Before he got inside the town he died, I must allow.
But since the town was won for us it is a lucky name,
And you'll remember Wolfe's good work, and you shall do the same."

Then Farmer said, "I'll try, sir," and Farmer bowed so low
That George could see his pigtail tied in a velvet bow.
George gave him his commission, and that it might be safer,
Signed "King of Britain, King of France," and sealed it with a wafer.

Then proud was Captain Farmer in a frigate of his own,
And grander on his quarter-deck than George upon his throne.
He'd two guns in his cabin, and on the spar-deck ten,
And twenty on the gun-deck, and more than ten score men.

And as a huntsman scours the brakes with sixteen brace of dogs,
With two-and-thirty cannon the ship explored the fogs.
From Cape la Hogue to Ushant, from Rochefort to Belleisle,
She hunted game till reef and mud were rubbing on her keel.

The fogs are dried, the frigate's side is bright with melting tar,
The lad up in the foretop sees square white sails afar;
The east wind drives three square-sailed masts from out the Breton bay,
And "Clear for action!" Farmer shouts, and reefers yell "Hooray!"

The Frenchmen's captain had a name I wish I could pronounce;
A Breton gentleman was he, and wholly free from bounce,
One like those famous fellows who died by guillotine
For honour and the fleurs-de-lys, and Antoinette the Queen.

The Catholic for Louis, the Protestant for George,
Each captain drew as bright a sword as saintly smiths could forge;
And both were simple seamen, but both could understand
How each was bound to win or die for flag and native land.

The French ship was *La Surveillante*, which means the watchful maid;
She folded up her head-dress and began to cannonade.
Her hull was clean, and ours was foul; we had to spread more sail.
On canvas, stays, and topsail yards her bullets came like hail.

Sore smitten were both captains, and many lads beside,
And still to cut our rigging the foreign gunners tried.
A sail-clad spar came flapping down athwart a blazing gun;
We could not quench the rushing flames, and so the
Frenchman won.

Our quarter-deck was crowded, the waist was all aglow;
Men clung upon the taffrail half scorched, but loth to go;
Our captain sat where once he stood, and would not quit his chair.
He bade his comrades leap for life, and leave him bleeding there.

The guns were hushed on either side, the Frenchmen lowered boats,
They flung us planks and hencoops, and everything that floats.
They risked their lives, good fellows! to bring their rivals aid.
'Twas by the conflagration the peace was strangely made.

La Surveillante was like a sieve; the victors had no rest.
They had to dodge the east wind to reach the port of Brest.
And where the waves leapt lower and the riddled ship went slower,
In triumph, yet in funeral guise, came fisher-boats to tow her.

They dealt with us as brethren, they mourned for Farmer dead;
And as the wounded captives passed each Breton bowed the head.
Then spoke the French Lieutenant, "'Twas fire that won, not we.
You never struck your flag to us; you'll go to England free."

'Twas the sixth day of October, seventeen hundred seventy-nine,
A year when nations ventured against us to combine, *Quebec* was burn
    and Farmer slain, by us remembered not;
But thanks be to the French book wherein they're not forgot.

Now you, if you've to fight the French, my youngster, bear in mind
Those seamen of King Louis so chivalrous and kind;
Think of the Breton gentlemen who took our lads to Brest,
And treat some rescued Breton as a comrade and a guest.

1885.

EPILOGUE.

Exactos, puer, esse decern tibi gratulor annos;
Hactenus es matris cura patrisque decus.
Incumbis studiis, et amas et amaris, et audes
Pro patria raucis obvius ire fretis.
Non erimus comites, fili, tibi; sed memor esto
Matris in oceano cum vigil astra leges.
Imbelli patre natus habe tamen arma Britannus,
Militiam perfer, spemque fidemque fove.

1889.

JE MAINTIENDRAI

(FOR THE TUNE CALLED SANTA LUCIA)

Rise, rise, ye Devon folk!
Toss off the traitor's yoke,
Peer through the rain and smoke,
Look, look again!
Run down to Brixham pier—
Quick, quick, the Prince is near!
All the rights ye reckon dear
He will maintain.

Chorus—
Welcome, sweet English rose!
Welcome, Dutch Roman nose!
Scatter, scatter all the Gospel's foes,
William and Mary!

High over gulls and boats
Bright, free the banner floats;
Hearken, hear the clarion notes!
Lift hats and stare.
Courtiers who break the laws,
Tame cats with velvet paws,

Hypocrites with poisoned claws,
Croppies, beware!

Trust, Sir, the western shires,
Trust those who baffled Spain;
We'll be hardy like our sires.
Down, Pope, again!
Off, off with sneak and thief!
We'll have an honest chief.
England is no Popish fief;
Free kings shall reign.

SAPPHICS FOR A TUNE

MADE BY REQUEST OF A
SONGSTRESS, AND REJECTED

Relics of battle dropt in sandy valley,
Bugle that screamed a warning of surprise,
Shreds of the colour torn before the rally,
Jewel of troth-plight seen by dying eyes—
Welcome, dear tokens of the lad we mourn.
Tell how that day his faithful heart was leaping;
Help me, who linger in the home forlorn,
Throw me a rainbow on my endless weeping.

1885.

JOHNNIE OF BRAIDISLEE

A SECOND ATTEMPT, ACCEPTED

Down the burnside hurry thee, gentle mavis,
Find the bothie, and flutter about the doorway.
Touch the lattice tenderly, bid my mother
Fetch away Johnnie.

Mother, uprouse thee! many bitter arrows
Out of one bosom gather, and for ever
Pray for one resting in a chilly forest
Under an oak tree.

Gentle mavis! hover about the window
Where the sun shines on happy things of home life,
Bid the clansmen troop to the gory dingle.
Clansmen, avenge me!

Mother! oh, my mother! upon a cradle
Woven of willows, with a bow beside me,
Near the kirk of Durrisdeer, under yew boughs,
Rock thy beloved.

1885.

EUROPA

May the foemen's wives, the foemen's children,
Feel the kid leaping when he lifts the surge,
Tumult of swart sea, and the reefs that shudder
Under the scourge.

On such a day to the false bull Europa
Trusted her snowy limbs; and courage failed her,
Where the whales swarmed, the terror of sea-change and
Treason assailed her.

For the meadow-fays had she duly laboured,
Eager for flowers to bind at eventide;
Shimmering night revealed the stars, the billows,
Nothing beside.

Brought to Crete, the realm of a hundred cities,
"Oh, my sire! my duty!" she clamoured sadly.
"Oh, the forfeit! and oh, the girl unfathered,
Wilfully, madly!

What shore is this, and what have I left behind me?
When a maid sins 'tis not enough to die.
Am I awake? or through the ivory gateway
Cometh a lie?

Cometh a hollow fantasy to the guiltless?
Am I in dreamland? Was it best to wander
Through the long waves, or better far to gather
Rosebuds out yonder?

Now, were he driven within the reach of anger,
Steel would I point against the villain steer,
Grappling, rending the horns of the bull, the monster
Lately so dear.

Shameless I left the homestead and the worship,
Shameless, 'fore hell's mouth, wide agape, I pause.
Hear me, some god, and set me among the lions
Stript for their jaws.

Ere on the cheek that is so fair to look on
Swoop the grim fiends of hunger and decay,
Tigers shall spring and raven, ere the sweetness
Wither away.

Worthless Europa! cries the severed father,
Why dost thou loiter, cling to life, and doat?
Hang on this rowan; hast thou not thy girdle
Meet for thy throat?

Lo, the cliff, the precipice, edged for cleaving,
Trust the quick wind, or take a leman's doom.
Live on and spin; thou wast a prince's daughter;
Toil at the loom.

Pass beneath the hand of a foreign lady;
Serve a proud rival." Lo, behind her back

Slyly laughed Venus, and her archer minion
Held the bow slack.

Then, the game played out, "Put away," she whispered,
"Wrath and upbraiding, and the quarrel's heat,
When the loathed bull surrenders horns, for riving,
Low at your feet.

Bride of high Jove's majesty, bride unwitting,
Cease from your sobbing; rise, your luck is rare.
Your name's the name which half the world divided
Henceforth shall bear."

HYPERMNESTRA

Let me tell Lydè of wedding-law slighted,
Penance of maidens and bootless task,
Wasting of water down leaky cask,
Crime in the prison-pit slowly requited.

Miscreant brides! for their grooms they slew.
One out of many is not attainted,
One alone blest and for ever sainted,
False to her father, to wedlock true.

Praise her! she gave her young husband the warning.
Praise her for ever! She cried, "Arise!
Flee from the slumber that deadens the eyes;
Flee from the night that hath never a morning.

Baffle your host who contrived our espousing,
Baffle my sisters, the forty and nine,
Raging like lions that mangle the kink,
Each on the blood of a quarry carousing.

I am more gentle, I strike not thee,
I will not hold thee in dungeon tower.
Though the king chain me, I will not cower,
Though my sire banish me over the sea.

Freely run, freely sail, good luck attend thee;
Go with the favour of Venus and Night.
On thy tomb somewhere and some day bid write
Record of her who hath dared to befriend thee."

BARINE

Lady, if you ever paid
Forfeit for a heart betrayed,
If for broken pledge you were
By one tooth, one nail less fair,

I would trust. But when a vow
Slips from off your faithless brow,
Forth you flash with purer lustre,
And a fonder troop you muster.

You with vantage mock the shade
Of a mother lowly laid,
Silent stars and depths of sky,
And high saints that cannot die.

Laughs the Queen of love, I say,
Laughs at this each silly fay,
Laughs the rogue who's ever whetting
Darts of fire on flint of fretting.

Ay, the crop of youth is yours,
Fresh enlistments throng your doors,
Veterans swear you serve them ill,
Threaten flight, and linger still.

Dames and thrifty greybeards dread
Lest you turn a stripling's head;
Poor young brides are in dismay
Lest you sigh their lords away.

TO BRITOMART MUSING

Classic throat and wrist and ear
Tempt a gallant to draw near;
Must romantic lip and eye
Make him falter, bid him fly?

If Camilla's upright lance
By the contrast did enhance
Charms of curving neck and waist,
Yet she never was embraced.

She was girt to take the field,
And her aventayle concealed
Half the grace that might have won
Homage from Evander's son.

Countess Montfort, clad in steel,
Showed she could both dare and feel;
Smiled to greet the champion ships,
Touched Sir Walter with the lips.

She could charm, although in dress
Like the sainted shepherdess,
Jeanne, a leader void of guile,
Jeanne, a woman all the while.

Damsel with the mind of man,
Lay not softness under ban;
For the glory of thy sex
Twine with myrtle manly necks.

HERSILIA

I see her stand with arms a-kimbo,
A blue and blonde *sub aureo nimbo*;
She scans her literary limbo,
The reliques of her teens;

Things like the chips of broken stilts,
Or tatters of embroidered quilts,
Or nosegays tossed away by jilts,
Notes, ballads, tales, and scenes.

Soon will she gambol like a lamb,
Fenced, but not tethered, near the Cam.
Maybe she'll swim where Byron swam,
And chat beneath the limes,

Where Arthur, Alfred, Fitz, and Brooks
Lit thought by one another's looks,
Embraced their jests and kicked their books,
In England's happier times;

Ere magic poets felt the gout,
Ere Darwin whelmed the Church in doubt
Ere Apologia had found out
The round world must be right;

When Gladstone, bluest of the blue,
Read all Augustine's folios through;
When France was tame, and no one knew
We and the Czar would fight.

"Sixty years since" (said dear old Scott;
We're bound, you know, to quote Sir Wat)
This isle had not a sweeter spot
Than Neville's Court by Granta;

No Newnham then, no kirtled scribes,
No Clelia to harangue the tribes,
No race for girls, no apple bribes
To tempt an Atalanta.

We males talked fast, we meant to be
World-betterers all at twenty-three,
But somehow failed to level thee,
Oh battered fort of Edom!

Into the breach our daughters press,
Brave patriots in unwarlike dress,
Adepts at thought-in-idleness,
Sweet devotees of freedom.

And now it is your turn, fair soul,
To see the fervent car-wheels roll,
Your rivals clashing past the goal,
Some sly Milanion leading.

Ah! with them may your Genius bring
Some Celia, some Miss Mannering;
For youthful friendship is a thing
More precious than succeeding.

SAPPHO'S CURSING

Woman dead, lie there;
No record of thee
Shall there ever be,
Since thou dost not share
Roses in Pieria grown.
In the deathful cave,
With the feeble troop
Of the folk that droop,
Lurk and flit and crave,
Woman severed and far-flown.

A SERVING MAN'S EPITAPH

A slave—oh yes, a slave!
But in a freeman's grave.
By thee, when work was done,
Timanthes, foster-son,
By thee whom I obeyed,
My master, I was laid.
Live long, from trouble free;
But if thou com'st to me,
Paying to age thy debt,
Thine am I, master, yet.

A SONG TO A SINGER

Dura fida rubecula,
Cur moraris in arbore
Dum cadunt folia et brevi
Flavet luce November.

Quid boni tibi destinât
Hora crastina? quid petes
Antris ex hiemalibus?
Quid speras oriturum?

Est ut hospita te vocet
Myrtis, et reseret fores,
Ut te vere nitentibus
Emiretur ocellis.

Quod si contigerit tibi,
Ter beata vocaberis,
Invidenda volucribus,
Invidenda poetæ.

AGE AND GIRLHOOD

ποιολογεῦσα κόρη ξηροῦ τέττιγος ἀκούει·

καὶ, τί κρέκεις, Τίθωνε; λέγει· μοχθῶ μὲν ἔγωγε,

σεῦ δὲ κλύειν πόνος ἐστιν ὁ δεύτερος· ἀλλ' ἀποκάμνειν

δεῖ με καθεζομένην ἀκρέσπερον· ἀγκὰς ἔχω τι·

εὐῶδες δὲ τὸ δράγμα· σὺ δ' εἶ κενὸς αὖος ἀτειρής.

A dry cicale chirps to a lass making hay,
"Why creak'st thou, Tithonus?" quoth she. "I don't play;
It doubles my toil, your importunate lay;
I've earned a sweet pillow, lo! Hesper is nigh;
I clasp a good wisp, and in fragrance I lie;
But thou art unwearied, and empty, and dry."

A LEGEND OF PORTO SANTO

A time-worn sage without a home,
A man of dim and tearful sight,
Up from the hallowed haven clomb
In lowly longing for the height.

He loiters on a half-way rock
To hear the waves that pant and seethe,
Which give the beats of Nature's clock
To mortals conscious that they breathe.

The buxom waves may nurse a boat,
May well nigh seem to soothe and lull
The crying of a tethered goat,
The trouble of a searching gull.

There might be comfort in the tide,
There might be Lethè in the surge,
Could they but hint that oceans hide,
That pangs absolve, bereavements purge.

The thinker, not despairing yet,
Upraises limbs not wholly stiff,
Half envying him that draws the net,
Half proud to combat with the cliff.

He groans, but soon around his lips
Tear-channels bend into a smile,
He thinks "They're saying in the ships
I'm looking for the hidden isle.

I climb but as my humours lead,
My thoughts are mazed, my will is faint,
Yon men who see me roam, they need
No Lethè-fount, no shriving saint."

Good faith! can we believe, or feign
Believing, that such lands exist
Through ages drenched with blotting rain,
For ever folded in the mist?

Maybe some babe by sirens clothed
Swam thence, and brought report thereof.
Some hopeful virgin just betrothed
Braved the incredulous pilot's scoff;

And murmuring to a friendly lute,
While greybeards snored and beldames laughed,
Some minstrel-corsair made pursuit
Along the moon's white hunting-shaft;

Along the straight illumined track
The bride, the singer, and the child
Fled, far from sceptics, came not back,
Engulped? Who knows? perhaps enisled.

Now were there such another crew,
Now would their bark make room for me,
Now were that island false or true,
I'd go, forgetting, with the three.

TO A LINNET

My cheerful mate, you fret not for the wires,
The changeless limits of your small desires;
You heed not winter rime or summer dew,
You feel no difference 'twixt old and new;
You kindly take the lettuce or the cress
Without the cognizance of more and less,
Content with light and movement in a cage.
Not reckoning hours, nor mortified by age,
You bear no penance, you resent no wrong,
Your timeless soul exists in each unconscious song.

A SONG FOR A PARTING

I.

Flora will pass from firth to firth;
Duty must draw, and vows must bind.
Flora will sail half round the earth,
Yet will she leave some grace behind.

II.

Waft her, on Faith, from friend to friend,
Make her a saint in some far isle;
Yet will we keep, till memories end,
Something that once was Flora's smile.

MIR IST LEIDE

Woe worth old Time the lord,
Pointing his senseless sword
Down on our festal board,
Where we would dine,
Chilling the kindly hall,
Bidding the dainties pall,
Making the garlands fall,
Souring the wine.

LEBEWOHL—WORDS FOR A TUNE

I.

With these words, Good-bye, Adieu
Take I leave to part from you,
Leave to go beyond your view,
Through the haze of that which is to be;
Fare thou forth, and wing thy way,
So our language makes me say.
Though it yield, the forward spirit needs must pray
In the word that is hope's old token.

II.

Though the fountain cease to play,
Dew must glitter near the brink,
Though the weary mind decay,
As of old it thought so must it think.
Leave alone the darkling eyes
Fixed upon the moving skies,
Cross the hands upon the bosom, there to rise
To the throb of the faith not spoken.

REMEMBER

οὐχ ἕρπεις παρὰ τύμβον ὁσημέραι, ὡς τὸ πάρος περ,
ὦ φίλ᾽, ἐγὼ δ᾽ ὁ θανὼν οὐ μέμφομαι, ὅττι τὺ παίσδεις.
ἀλλ᾽ ὁπόταν παίσδῃς, μέμνασό γε τοῦ πρὶν ἑταίρου,
κεἴ τι καλὸν ποθόρησθα, μόνον λέγε, τῆνος ἄπεστι.

You come not, as aforetime, to the headstone every day,
And I, who died, I do not chide because, my friend, you play;
Only, in playing, think of him who once was kind and dear,
And, if you see a beauteous thing, just say, he is not here.

APPENDIX

TO THE INFALLIBLE

("Ionica," 1858, p. 60)

Old angler, what device is thine
To draw my pleasant friends from me?
Thou fishest with a silken line
Not the coarse nets of Galilee.

In stagnant vivaries they lie,
Forgetful of their ancient haunts;
And how shall he that standeth by
Refrain his open mouth from taunts?

How? by remembering this, that he,
Like them, in eddies whirled about,
Felt less: for thus they disagree:
He can, they could not, bear to doubt.

THE SWIMMER'S WISH

("Ionica," 1858, p. 81)

Fresh from the summer wave, under the beech,
Looking through leaves with a far-darting eye,
Tossing those river-pearled locks about,
Throwing those delicate limbs straight out,
Chiding the clouds as they sailed out of reach,
Murmured the swimmer, I wish I could fly.

Laugh, if you like, at the bold reply,
Answer disdainfully, flouting my words:
How should the listener at simple sixteen
Guess what a foolish old rhymer could mean
Calmly predicting, "You will surely fly"—
Fish one might vie with, but how be like birds?

Sweet maiden-fancies, at present they range
Close to a sister's engarlanded brows,
Over the diamonds a mother will wear,
In the false flowers to be shaped for her hair.—
Slow glide the hours to thee, late be the change,
Long be thy rest 'neath the cool beechen boughs!

Genius and love will uplift thee: not yet,
Walk through some passionless years by my side,
Chasing the silly sheep, snapping the lily stalk,
Drawing my secrets forth, witching my soul with talk.
When the sap stays, and the blossom is set,
Others will take the fruit, I shall have died.

AN APOLOGY

("Ionica," 1858, p. 115)

Uprose the temple of my love
Sculptured with many a mystic theme,
All frail and fanciful above,
But pillared on a deep esteem.

It might have been a simpler plan,
And traced on more majestic lines;
But he that built it was a man
Of will unstrung, and vague designs;

Not worthy, though indeed he wrought
With reverence and a meek content,
To keep that presence: yet the thought
Is there, in frieze and pediment.

The trophied arms and treasured gold
Have passed beneath the spoiler's hand;
The shrine is bare, the altar cold,
But let the outer fabric stand.

NOTRE DAME—
FROM THE SOUTH-EAST

("Ionica," 1877)

Oh lord of high compassion, strong to scorn
Ephemeral monsters, who with tragic pain
Purgest our trivial humours, once again
Through thine own Paris have I roamed, to mourn

For freemen plagued with cant, ere we were born,
For feasts of death, and hatred's harvest wain
Piled high, for princes from proud mothers torn,
And soft despairs hushed in the waves of Seine.

Oh Victor, oh my prophet, wilt thou chide
If Gudule's pangs, and Marion's frustrate plea,
And Gauvrain's promise of a heavenly France,
Thy sadly worshipt creatures, almost died
This evening, for that spring was on the tree,
And April dared in children's eyes to dance?

April 1877.

IN HONOUR OF MATTHEW PRIOR

ψιλὸν ὁρᾷς τὸ κάτοπτρον ἐπεί μ' ἐτεχνήσατο κεῖνος,

ὅσπερ τῆσδε κόρης οἶδε τίς ἐστὶ φυή.

οὐ στέφος, οὐ ποίκιλμα φέρω βύσσου τε λίθων τε·

μή σε γ' ἀνιάτω, φησί, πρόσωπον ἔχεις.

("Ionica," 1877)

I am Her mirror, framed by him
Who likes and knows her. On my rim
No fret, no bead, no lace.
He tells me not to mind the scorning
Of every semblance of adorning,
Since I receive Her face.

Sept. 1877.

The following little Greek lyric occurs in a letter of December 18
1862, to the Rev. E. D. Stone. "My lines," wrote William Johnson, "are
suggested by the death of Thorwaldsen: he died at the age of seventy
imperceptibly, having fallen asleep at a concert. But when I had done

hem, I remembered Provost Hawtrey's last appearance in public at a music party, where he fell asleep: and so I value my lines as a bit of honour done to him, and it seems odd that I should unintentionally have caught in the second and third lines his characteristic sympathy with the young . . ."

NEC CITHARA CARENTEM

γῆρας οὐ σὲ πρέπει, Μνημοσύνης παῖ λιγυρά, στυγεῖν,
ἥτις οἶσθα Χρόνον τοῖς αγαθοῖς ὡς θεὸς εὐμαρής,
καὶ Πλάτωνι σύνει καὶ Σοφοκλεῖ, κοὐκ αριθμεῖς ἔτη.

δεῦρ' Ἐλευθερίᾳ σύννομε καὶ μῆτερ ἀηδόνων·
ὦτά μοι μέλος οὐ λαμπρὸν ἔδυ· νῦν δ' ἀπερεῖν δοκῶ
οὐκ ἄνευ σέθεν, εἴθ' ὕπνος ὅδ' ἐστ' εἴτε τὸ τεθνάναι.

Guide me with song, kind Muse, to death's dark shade;
Keep me in sweet accord with boy and maid,
Still in fresh blooms of art and truth arrayed.

Bear with old age, blithe child of memory!
Time loves the good; and youth and thou art nigh
To Sophocles and Plato, till they die.

Playmate of freedom, queen of nightingales,
Draw near; thy voice grows faint: my spirit fails
Still with thee, whether sleep or death assails.

9 781016 367599